ME MAM. ME DAD. ME.

MALCOLM DUFFY is a Geordie, born and bred. His first novel, *Me Mam. Me Dad. Me.*, was inspired by his time at Comic Relief, visiting projects that support women and children who have suffered as a result of domestic abuse. Malcolm lives in Surrey with wife Jann, and daughters Tallulah and Tabitha. He works as an advertising copywriter.

Me Mam.
Me Dad.
M E.

Malcolm Duffy

ZEPHYR

First published in the UK in 2018 by Zephyr,
an imprint of Head of Zeus Ltd

9 7 5 3 1 2 4 6 8

A catalogue record for this book is available from
the British Library.

ISBN (HB): 9781786697646
ISBN (E): 9781786697639

Typeset by Adrian McLaughlin

Printed and bound in Great Britain by
CPI Group (UK) Ltd, Croydon CRO 4YY

Head of Zeus Ltd
First Floor East
5–8 Hardwick Street
London ECIR 4RG

WWW.HEADOFZEUS.COM

For me mam

One

•

It was the day the clocks went back. That's when I decided to kill him.

I'd been playing football with me mates, Barry Mossman, Ben Simpson and Carl Hedgley from school. Gavin Latham should have been there too but his mam took him for a haircut. We were in the park near the cemetery. Just did corners and penalties. You can't have a proper game with four.

It got too dark to see the ball. Told Barry he should have brought his white one. So we went home. I normally go on me bike, but it had a flatty. Bounced me ball all the way. Three hundred and eighty-seven bounces it was. Counted them. Nearly gave up a few times, but it gave me something to do.

Went round the side of the house, through the gate and in the back door. Mam always leaves it open when I'm out. The second I opened the door I heard it – crying, big crying like you hear on the telly sometimes. Thought at first maybe it was the telly. Put the ball next to the pedal bin, went to the front room, and peeped in. The telly was off. Black. Nobody there.

Stood still for a bit and listened. The crying was coming from upstairs. Sounded a bit like me mam, but was weird, quiet one minute and dead loud the next, like someone was messing with the volume. Went slow to the top of the stairs. Crept to her door on tippy-toes and listened. That's where it was coming from. Was her all right, definitely her. The noise made me guts feel funny, like I was on a roller coaster. Had a feeling I knew what had happened. Hoped I was wrong. I needed to find out. Took a breath and turned the handle.

Locked.

Who puts a lock on a bedroom door?

Knocked.

'Mam.'

The crying was too big.

'Mam, it's Danny. What's the marra?' I shouted.

The crying stopped, dead quick.

'Go downstairs, Danny,' she screamed. The way her voice sounded scared me more than the crying.

'Y'alreet, Mam?'

Stupid question.

'Yes.'

Stupid answer.

'Course she wasn't all right. You don't cry like that when you're all right. Not unless there's something really sad on telly. Or somebody's dead. Or a pet.

'Have you hurt yourself?'

'Go away, Danny, please.'

Wanted to.

Didn't.

'What's happened?'

'Nothing.'

But I knew it was something. Not even a cissy cries like that, and me mam's not one of those. I saw her shout at a bloke in the supermarket once. Was next to the crisps. He had tattoos all over his bald head. He'd bashed her trolley but never said sorry, just eyeballed her. She shouted at him and crossed her arms. Wouldn't back down. I was dead proud of her.

'Do you want a cup of tea, Mam?'

Never heard her say no to a cup of tea.

'No.'

Weird.

'Where's Callum?'

I heard a laugh. But it was the type you do when something's not funny.

'Where do you think?' she said.

Knew the answer to that one.

'Shall I call Aunty Tina?'

'No.'

'Uncle Greg?'

'No'

'What about Uncle Martin?'

'No,' shouted me mam, even louder. 'I want you to go away.'

And then the crying started again.

I just wanted to know what had happened, that's all, but she's me mam so I did as I was told. Went downstairs and turned on the telly. Hoped there might be football on, but couldn't find any anywhere. Must have been my unlucky day, there's always football on somewhere. Found another channel, with lions. I like lions, me. They were scrapping. I turned the sound up. The fighting drowned out me mam.

It was tea time. But there was no tea. This was the first time this had happened. Ever. Mam always makes me tea, even when she's got the flu or had too much red wine. But for once I was glad she'd not made any. I wasn't hungry. You can't eat when your guts are clenched as tight as a fist. Not when you don't know what's happened to your mam.

I got bored with the lions pawing each other and called Amy. Just hearing her voice would make me feel better. But her phone was off. I left a message saying I hoped she was okay.

Looked out of the window. It was dark outside now, really dark. That's what happens when you change the clocks. Stupid idea if you ask me. Why would you want it to be dark at tea time one day when the day before it wasn't? Doesn't make a scrap of sense. I watched some more telly. This time I turned the sound off so I could listen for me mam. Rugby was on. Don't like rugby. It's even more stupid with the sound off.

Just when I thought nothing would ever happen, it did. I heard soft footsteps on the stairs, like a burglar would make. It was me mam, coming to make me tea.

'Mam?'

'Stay in there, son,' she said. 'Just stay in there, please.'

I heard her slippers shuffling to the kitchen, like she was dragging something heavy. Then she blew her nose.

She'd told me to stay put, but I couldn't. Had to know. Opened the door dead quiet and went in slow motion down the hall. The kitchen door was shut. I was scared, like watching a horror film, when you don't know what's in the room. I turned the handle, pushed the door a bit, and peeped in.

Me mam was just standing there, her back to me, looking out into the dark. But she didn't have to turn.

I saw her face mirrored in the window, covered in great big bruises, one of her eyes as black as the sky outside.

She reached across, grabbed a kitchen towel, and spat into it. The white paper turned red.

Mam slumped over the sink, her arms across her stomach like she had a cramp, and started crying again.

That's when I knew I had to kill him.

Two

• •

I love me mam, me.

Just as well. For years we'd been living together in the same flat. No relatives. No boyfriend. No bairns. No lodgers. Just us.

I reckon she'd do anything for me. Always got something lush to microwave for me tea. Always lets me go on her laptop. Always makes sure me football kit's clean. Socks the right way round. Always buys me the top thing off me birthday list, even though I know she's not minted. And always gives me a goodnight hug, even when I've done nowt to deserve it. Bet there's not many mams do all that.

I think I drive her mad sometimes, but she usually just folds her arms and blows out hot air. She hardly ever goes mental. I get shouted at enough at school, so it's good to live in a shout-free zone.

I bet she secretly wishes she had a daughter. But if she does she never lets on. Just has to listen to me football talk with her wish-he'd-talk-about-something-else-face. The same face I've got when she talks about clothes.

But me mam's not just kind, she's also dead pretty. Short, but pretty. I reckon she could be a model if it wasn't for the chocolate biscuits. But can't see her ever ditching them. They're her number one drug.

'Danny, take them away from me,' she says.

If she doesn't want them, why does she get them out in the first place?

So instead of being a model, she works in a call centre. She's got a canny voice, me mam. Think that's how she got her job.

When I was little me mam and me used to live with me gran and granda down the road in Dunston. I liked living there. It was a house with people always coming and going. Neighbours, friends, relatives, they'd all pop in for any reason whatsoever and the house would be full of noise. Me gran's one of those people who never runs out of things to say. If talking was in the Olympics she'd win a gold.

But when I was about nine we had to leave.

'We're gonna have to move, Danny. We've outgrown this place.'

Me mam and me used to share the same room. Said now that I was bigger it was time we got our own place. So she went and got a flat off the council in Low Fell.

The council have got millions of flats and houses. I don't know why they had to go and give us that one. It wasn't like me gran's house. No garden. No upstairs. It just had four rooms. Five, if you count the toilet. It got that cold in the winter me mam and me would get dressed for going out, even when we were stopping in. And the walls got wet for no good reason. But it had two good things about it. I had me own bedroom, and it was near me school, so I could stop in bed till the very last second.

We didn't get many people coming to our flat. Maybe me mam didn't have enough chairs. Or maybe she was embarrassed about the temperature or the wet. I missed all the people who used to come to me gran's. And I don't see so much of her and granda now. Shame. Love me gran almost as much as me mam. She's dead huggy. Love me granda too. But he doesn't give any hugs. He's got dementia.

But I still got to see everyone. Whenever it was a birthday or something we'd all get together for a party at me mam's sister's house. Aunty Tina's different from me mam. She's got a car, a swanky house and a posh voice. Aunty Tina doesn't live round here. She lives over the Tyne in a place that's that big they need a cleaner. Uncle Greg must have the best job ever. Or he's a criminal. They've got two bairns, Tabitha and Marcus. Also posh.

Then there's the relatives we don't see much, like me mam's cousins who live in Manchester, and her brother, Uncle Martin, who lost his job and went to live in Darlington with Aunty Sheila. They haven't got any bairns. Maybe that's why they're so happy when they see me. Like people who haven't got a dog, when they see a dog.

Aye, me life with me mam wasn't the sort you'd make a film about, but it was canny. I had me mates. I had me football. I had me relatives. I had me mam. She loved me. I loved her. Was happy for that to go on and on and on and on.

And then me world went upside down.

Three

• • •

Can't exactly remember when he showed up, he just did. About a year ago, I think.

Me mam found him on her computer. One minute he wasn't there, then he was. I didn't want to kill him, not back then. It was good, at first. He seemed sort of ordinary, just a normal bloke.

He was big, with massive hands, saggy chin, and a belly that flopped right over the top of his belt like a duvet off the edge of the bed. His voice wasn't from round here, down south somewhere, maybe London. He had dark, curly hair, two little blue eyes, and a big mouth to go with his big chin. He also had a very smiley face. I remember that the first time I saw him, a cheesy grin, wide, like he was always taking selfies. His name was Callum Jeffries.

I don't know what he was doing up our way. Never asked him. He told me he worked in computers. I think he might have been the boss. He had quick fingers, fat, but quick. Me mam's not that good on computers. I'm better than her, but Callum was better than me. S'pose he should be. It's his job.

He didn't move in. Hardly enough room for me and me mam. So they used to go out to the pub, the pictures, the coast, wherever.

Me mam fancied Callum like mad. Always holding hands and stroking each other's arms and legs, gazing at each other, like they'd discovered something amazing. When he wasn't there she'd call him, putting on that phone voice she's got, like you hear on the adverts, making people buy stuff they don't really want. And at night they'd lie on our little sofa with their legs and arms all tangled together like wrestlers or octopuses or ropes.

I was happy me mam was happy.

Callum was dead friendly when he first turned up. He'd pat me head like I was a bairn and give me money and say, 'There you go, General.' Mam would try and stop him, but he'd do it anyway.

He'd only been round me mam's a few times when

he asked if I wanted to go for a drive in his car, a massive Range Rover.

Said aye.

We crossed the river and went up to Hadrian's Wall. Callum said he'd always wanted to drive down a proper Roman road. The Romans would have put in a few speed bumps if they'd known he was coming.

'Prepare for take-off, General.'

He floored the accelerator and we shot off like a firework. Never seen anyone drive that fast before. The Romans couldn't be bothered with boring things like roundabouts and bends. They made their roads dead straight, like the lines on a football pitch. I sneaked a peek at the speedo. A hundred and five miles per hour.

'Yee-hah,' he shouted, as we overtook a van like it was parked.

Callum was loving every second.

We hit one of the dips and I swear me stomach ended up among me brains. Was the maddest car journey I'd ever been on in me life.

'Not scared, are you, General?'

'No.'

Yes.

'Bet you can't wait till you can do that?'

Bet I can.

Don't know why he needed to drive that fast. Not even like he was late for something. But he did it anyway.

'Did you boys have a nice trip?' said me mam, when we got back.

'Aye, canny.'

'Think the General wants to be a test pilot.'

And we all laughed. But me laugh was made up. I wasn't a hundred per cent sure what to make of me mam's new bloke. Think he wanted us to be mates, what with the money, and the hair rubbing, and the car ride and calling me General. Like he really wanted me to like him.

One weekend Callum took us up to his house in Whickham. Was belter. Callum had a double garage, a garden front and back, and nobody living on top or right next to him. Reckoned he must have the world's fastest computer fingers to afford a place like that.

I could tell me mam loved it too, opening and closing all the shiny drawers and cupboards, grinning, like she was watching kittens on the internet.

'Lovely, isn't it, Danny?' she said.

'Aye, top.'

Couldn't believe she'd found herself a bloke with all this. Maybe it was her voice that did it.

We went in his kitchen. It was bigger than our front room.

'What's that do?' I said, pointing to a funny-looking tap.

'It does water; still water, sparkling water and boiling water,' went Callum. 'Genius, eh?'

'You'd love one of them, Mam,' I said. 'The amount of tea you drink.'

'Cheeky beggar.' Then gave me a hug to show she didn't mean it.

But the best thing in the house was in the front room. Callum's telly. It was that big it nearly covered a whole wall. I swear I've seen smaller screens down the Metro Centre. Think Callum spotted me poppy-out eyes. He turned it on and gave me the remote. It had all the channels we couldn't afford.

'Bet you'd love to watch the Toon on that, wouldn't you?' said me mam.

Too right.

We did a tour of the rest of the house. I normally can't think of much to say about houses, they're just rooms, but had to admit that this place was even better than Aunty Tina's. I'd never seen me mam so excited, apart from when she sees shoes.

The house was spotless, like nobody lived here. I imagine it was the sort of place you'd get screamed at if you dared come in with clarty shoes. Callum must be mad on cleaning.

I also found out something else about him. He was a bit of a joker.

Me mam was downstairs working her way through his chocolate biscuits.

'You wanna watch yourself, girl,' he said.

'What do you mean?'

'That bum of yours. I've seen elephants with smaller backsides.'

And me and Callum laughed.

Four

• •

A funny thing happened.

Not funny ha, ha, more like funny fantastic.

Not long after me mam found herself a boyfriend, I went and found meself a girlfriend. I hadn't really been looking for one. She just sort of showed up.

I was wheeling me bike through the school gates one day when Amy Reynolds came over.

'Hi, Danny,' she went.

Couldn't figure out why Amy was talking to me. She's cool and cheeky and the third prettiest lass in class. She's got shortish, blondish hair, blue eyes, and a smile that proves she's got an electric toothbrush. I fancied her that much that I never really spoke to her.

'What you doing?' she said.

'Pushing me bike. Otherwise it'll fall over.'

Amy laughed, and started walking beside me.

Wasn't sure what to do next. I could get on me bike, but I'd have to ride that slow I'd probably fall off. I decided to keep pushing it. Just having her that close was making me feel horny, me heart bashing away so fast I could feel it in me ears.

'Do you fancy going to the pictures on Saturday?' she said.

Nearly dropped me bike.

'Me?'

'No, I'm talking to me imaginary friend.' She let loose a sigh. 'Yes, of course you, Danny.'

Could feel me face go hot.

'Aye, that would be canny,' I said, trying to make it sound like it was no big deal, when actually it was the biggest deal ever. I was being asked out by *Amy Reynolds*. *The Amy Reynolds*. Belter.

'I'll meet you outside the cinema at the Metro Centre, one o'clock.'

I hoped she might have gone for a later screening. Newcastle were live on telly, twelve-thirty kick-off.

'Aye, perfect,' I lied.

'See you then, Danny,' said Amy, and walked off, calm as you like.

I stood stock still, frozen like a lolly. I didn't even know that Amy liked me. I mean, I'd seen her smile at me a few times. I didn't for one second think it meant anything, that she wasn't just smiling, she was thinking about me, having the same thoughts about me as I was having about her. Well, probably not that dirty.

Then Barry elbowed me in the ribs.

'What's up with ye, man? Look like you've seen a ghost.'

'Just daydreaming,' I said, as I watched Amy walking away.

Barry saw where me eyes had gone. 'Dream on, Danny, dream on. You have absolutely no chance.'

I tried to stop a smile coming. But couldn't.

Saturday couldn't come round fast enough. But it finally showed up and I caught the bus to the Metro Centre. Didn't tell me mam where I was going. In fact, I didn't tell anyone where I was going. Just in case the trip was a disaster. Also, felt a bit bad that Amy had gone and asked me out. I mean, isn't that the lad's job? If Barry or anyone asks, I'd say that I'd been planning it for ages.

I walked through the crowds and spotted Amy trying to spot me. She looked nothing like the Amy Reynolds from school. High heels, make-up, leather jacket and jeans so tight even Tony Heskill, the randiest kid in class, couldn't get his hands inside them. I think she'd done something to her hair too. I decided not to say anything, though, just in case she hadn't.

I don't normally dress smart when I go to the cinema. Not much point when it's dark inside. But today was different. I'd polished me shoes, found me best jeans, and put on the shirt me mam makes me wear at parties.

'Hi, Danny. You look nice.'

'And you look excellent.' Don't know where that word came from, but Amy seemed happy with me adjective and smiled.

I wanted to kiss her, but there were too many people about. Also, I'd have to go right up on tippy-toes. Like just about everyone else in class, Amy's a lot taller than me. With her high heels on, it was like being with a giant, a gorgeous giant. I gave her a quick hug, the type you give your teammate when he's just scored.

We went and watched the film, but to be honest I couldn't tell you much about it, because being that close to Amy made it impossible to concentrate. We'd both taken our jackets off and our bare elbows were touching on the armrest. I know elbow-touching isn't exactly porn. Never seen it in any of the films we watch on Barry's phone. But I swear the warmth I could feel from Amy's elbow made me hornier than I've ever felt in me entire life.

When the film finished we went outside.

'That was good,' said Amy.

I wasn't sure whether she meant the film or the elbow-touching.

'Aye, dead good.'

Then Amy stood close to me. Incredibly close. I didn't think it was possible to feel happy, excited and sick all at the same time, but I did. This is it, I thought. She's going to kiss me. Down the Metro Centre.

'Shall we get a hot chocolate?' she said.

Oh, well.

'Aye,' I said, trying hard to sound enthusiastic. 'Hot chocolate would be fantastic.'

We walked together through the shoppers and found a café. I was that happy being with Amy I'd even forgotten to check how the Toon had got on. Amy grabbed a table and I went and got us two hot chocolates. After taking a sip, Amy stared into me eyes, like she was trying to hypnotise me. Amy had the most beautiful eyes of any girl in Year Eight. Right now, I almost wished she didn't. I had the biggest stiffy ever.

'Can you get me a spoon?' asked Amy.

Wazzocks.

Why didn't I wear me long jacket?

'A spoon?'

'Aye. To stir me drink.'

Me brain was on holiday. Couldn't think of a single

way to get out of me predicament. Before Amy thought I was a total nutter, an idea slipped into me head.

'Is that Chloe over there?' I said.

Amy turned to look and I tipped me drink over.

'Oh, man,' I said, looking at the pool of chocolate, now dripping off the edge of the table into me lap.

Amy jumped up and came back with some serviettes for me, and a spoon for her. I glanced down. It looked like I'd cacked the front of me jeans.

'What happened?' said Amy.

I got dead excited sitting opposite you. So to avoid the embarrassment of seeing me walk like a hunchback through the café to get your spoon I poured hot chocolate into me crotch.

'Nothing.'

Wiped me jeans as best I could.

Amy stirred her drink. Then she reached across the table and touched me hand.

'I really like you, Danny. You're cute.'

I thought cute was what puppies got called, but I wasn't going to go all English teacher on her: *'Reynolds, can't you come up with a better word than that?'* Cute was fine by me.

'Thanks. I think you're cute too,' I said, me voice going high like me mam's.

I wasn't exactly sure what to do next, so I grinned. Must have been the right thing to do, because Amy took me other hand.

'Tell me something about you that I don't know,' said Amy.

The heat from Amy's hands was making it hard to think straight.

'I can do twenty-six keepy-uppies with a ball.'

'No, something more personal.'

Not sure what she meant, but I gave it a crack.

'There's just me mam and me in our family. But me mam's got herself a new boyfriend.'

'That's nice.'

'Aye, he seems like a canny bloke. Calls me General.'

'You're not going to war, are you?'

'Too small for that. There's bullets taller than me.'

'You're funny, Danny.'

Glad she thought so. I reckoned I was talking pants.

'Now tell *me* something personal,' I said.

Amy put a different face on.

'I think I might have found a boyfriend.'

Had that little spit in me mouth I could barely speak.

'Really?'

'It's a bit embarrassing, but he's called General.'

She leaned across the table. Our noses bumped but our lips managed to find each other.

I'd gone and got meself a girlfriend.

Five

•

I told me mam about Amy.

She was dead happy for me. Asked loads of questions. She must have liked me answers 'cos she just stood there, smiling. And then the smile disappeared.

'Just don't do anything stupid, Danny.'

Knew what she meant.

Not long after I started going out with Amy, we moved into Callum's house.

I was a bit sorry to be leaving our old flat. Although it was like living inside a fridge, something inside me quite liked it. But there's no going back. Someone else lives there now. You've got to move on. That's what me mam says.

I wanted to see Amy the day we moved out, but Mam said there was plenty of time for that. She needed me help.

'Alreet, Mam,' I said.

Didn't want to start a fight.

Callum hired a van to move our stuff, but most of it didn't even make it to his place. Ended up in the tip. No point in having crappy furniture in a nice new house like that. It took us about five goes to get it all done. By the end I was knackered. Callum stuffed a tenner in me pocket. 'That's your moving-in present, General,' he said, rubbing me hair.

'Ta.'

Then me mam went to the shops to get some food.

'Fancy going to the park?' said Callum.

'Aye.'

Went and got me ball.

Callum was rubbish at football. He couldn't control it. Like he'd never seen one before.

'Which team do you support?' I said.

'Don't.'

Explained everything.

He said he liked Formula One. Said I didn't. We didn't talk much after that.

He got too puffed for football and went to sit on a bench to fiddle with his phone. I practised corners.

When we got back me mam was putting stuff away in the kitchen.

'Have you unpacked your boxes, Danny?'

'Na.'

'Well, don't expect me to do it. I want your bedroom tidy from now on. This is a gorgeous house. Let's keep it that way.'

'I'll do it later.'

'You'll do it now.'

But it wasn't just me mam who got cross that day. It was also the first time I saw Callum go mental, I mean, totally mental. After unpacking the last of the boxes, he said, 'That's enough work for one day, let's go and get some fish and chips.'

We were in his car on the road to Cullercoats when a driver came out of a side road and just missed us. Callum swerved, then braked hard, sending us forwards and backwards like ragdolls.

'Maniac,' screamed Callum.

The driver was a young lass. Not that Callum cared. He went chasing after her like he was a copper. Got really close behind her, flashing his lights.

'Callum,' went me mam.

But he wasn't listening. I could see his mouth in the rear-view mirror. The smile had vanished, his lips clamped shut like a computer lid.

'Stop,' said me mam. 'Please stop'.

But he didn't, he just went faster and faster and overtook the lass. Got right in front, then braked. Slam.

Didn't have me seat belt on, and bashed me nose hard into Mam's headrest. It hurt like stink.

Callum got out and went over to the lass's car, shaking his fists and using all the swear words he could think of. He kicked her door with his massive shoe. I thought she'd be dead scared. Thought wrong. She got out of the car and started screaming back at him.

'How dare you do that?' she shouted. 'I was indicating to come out. You were the one who was speeding. You need driving lessons.'

Callum gave her the finger, got back in, then drove off really fast, like he was in a race.

'And that, Danny, is why a woman will never win Formula One,' he said, laughing.

We got some fish and chips. They were lush. But I noticed me mam didn't eat much. She and Callum didn't talk much either. Just looked out at the flat sea.

When we got back from the coast I went to me room and did as Mam said and tried to make it tidy.

Later on saw me mam and Callum cuddling in the hall. She must have forgiven him for going mental. Then Callum decided to have a party, a moving-in party. He turned the music up dead loud, got crisps and nuts and beer and stuff, and me mam and Callum had a dance in the kitchen. Was funny to watch. Him throwing his big arms about like he'd had enough of them, and me mam doing tiny little moves like she was trapped in an invisible box. I was happy to see her laughing and dancing. Can't remember the last time I'd seen that. Think it was Aunty Tina's house after Tabitha's christening.

Me mam finally flopped on to a chair, face all red, like she'd just done cross-country.

'I'm ready for bed,' she said.

'But we haven't had the champagne yet,' said Callum, grabbing a bottle from the fridge.

'Save it for another day.'

'No, it's for today, our big day,' he said. 'I bought it specially.'

'I don't want any.'

'Is there something wrong with your hearing? I said it's our special day,' he went, his voice going school-teachery.

He took the foil off and shook the bottle. The cork flew out and just missed me mam's head.

'Callum,' she went.

But if he was sorry, he didn't act it. He just sprayed champagne over her, like they do at the end of Formula One. Me mam wasn't happy, not one bit, wiping her dress down with a tea towel, her face all grumpy, as Callum laughed.

He poured champagne into a glass and handed it to her. She pushed it away.

'I've poured you a drink, so drink it,' he said, his face right up close to hers.

Me mam took the glass with a shaky hand and had a sip. Even though she wanted to go to bed. Even though she didn't want a drink.

That was the day we moved in.

Six

• • •

Christmas Day. Won't forget that one in a hurry.

In the morning we got that many presents I thought Callum must have robbed a bank. I got a brand new mountain bike, me first-ever mobile phone, a Toon hoodie, a camera, football shorts, and best of all, a goal for the back garden. When it was just me mam and me I used to get one good present, a bar of chocolate and a hug.

Mam got tons of stuff too. Perfume, clothes, belts, necklaces, the lot.

'You shouldn't have,' she said.

'Okay, I'll take them back tomorrow.'

They both laughed and then locked on, mouths open, like they were giving each other the kiss of life. It went on that long I had to leave.

Got dressed and went on me new bike down Whickham Bank to Amy's house. Her place was a bit smaller than Callum's, but canny enough. Her mam opened the door. She was wearing checked pyjama trousers, a fluffy jumper with a flashing snowman on the front, and a funny hat. Christmas makes people dress dead funny.

'Merry Christmas, Danny,' she said, and gave me a hug and a kiss.

I like Amy's mam and dad. They never seem to be in a bad mood. Unless they save it till I'm gone. They also seemed happy that I was going out with Amy. At least that's what she told me.

'Come on in,' she said.

I left me new bike parked against their front wall. Don't think thieves would steal a bike on Christmas Day. Too busy opening all the presents they've nicked.

'Amy's just upstairs getting ready. Would you like a drink, or a mince pie, Danny?'

'No, thanks, Mrs Reynolds.'

I waited in their front room. It was about as Christmassy as you can get. Sleigh bell music coming from somewhere, a bushy tree covered in tinsel, fire going, and Amy's nine-year-old brother, Tyler, and four-year-old sister, Ellie, playing on the floor with their presents. Made me wish I had a brother or sister.

A couple of minutes later I heard feet racing down the stairs.

'Merry Christmas, Danny,' said Amy, as she dashed in, all smiley.

She looked even more gorgeous than normal. I wanted to hug her tight, but her brother and sister were staring at us, waiting to see what we'd do next.

'Let's go outside,' she said.

She grabbed me hand and we went through the kitchen, which was starting to smell of turkey, out of the back door and into the alleyway down the side of the house. There was a little garden shed there. Amy opened the door and pulled me in.

It was packed full of gardening stuff. But there was just enough room for me and Amy to squeeze together. Close.

Never thought I'd get excited being in a garden shed, but I was now.

After school Amy and me usually hung round the back of The Immaculate Heart of Mary. There's nowhere else in Gateshead you're less likely to meet anyone from school. We'd hold hands, and she'd give me titchy pecks on the lips, the sort you'd give your gran. But that was it. I reckoned it was because Amy was a Catholic.

But something about the look on her face told me that she wasn't after granny pecks today.

'Here's your present,' I said, pulling a little package from under me jumper.

I'd got her some perfume. Not that she needs any. She always smells lush.

'Oh, Danny. That's brilliant,' said Amy, tearing off the wrapper and looking at the little bottle.

'And I've got something for you.'

With a spark in her eyes she backed me into a corner by the lawnmower and gave me the biggest kiss ever. Without any warning she had her tongue in me mouth, her hands up the back of me jumper, and her perfume up me nose. It was like she'd taken over me entire body. If I went through every word in the dictionary I couldn't find one to describe how I felt. The French have probably got one. But I'm useless at that.

I wanted the kiss to go on forever and ever.

'Amy,' shouted her mam, from the back door. 'I need your help with the sprouts.'

Amy rubbed her neck. Must have been stiff from all that bending down. Me whole body was now twitching. Even me brain felt funny, like the time me and Barry drank his dad's beer.

'Merry Christmas, Danny,' she said.

I cycled back home with a grin bigger than anything Callum could come up with. I wished I could have stayed in Amy's shed all day, but I couldn't. We were going to Aunty Tina and Uncle Greg's for Christmas lunch.

Aunty Tina and Uncle Greg live in Darras Hall, near the airport. It's where people with tons of money live, like footballers. Some of the houses are that big you can't even see them from the road. You don't see any rubbish in the street either, and people bend down to pick up their dog poo. It's that sort of place.

We got there in about two minutes. Callum was driving.

It was also dead Christmassy in me aunt and uncle's house, like walking into Santa's grotto. All me relatives from the North East were there.

Gave me gran a giant hug.

'Merry Christmas, Danny,' she went.

'Y'alreet, Granda?' I said, touching his hand.

But he said nothing. Don't think he even knew it was Christmas.

Uncle Martin and Aunty Sheila both squeezed me hard. And Uncle Greg shook my hand. Like it was the end of a match. They also made a fuss of Callum. None of them had met him before. And I think they liked what they saw. He chatted away like me gran.

We swapped presents and hugs. Then it was time for lunch. They sat me down the end of the table with Tabitha and Marcus, which was about as bad a punishment as I could think of.

'Danny, put that phone away,' said me mam.

'What's the point of having a phone if I can't use it?'

'We're at lunch. It's when people are meant to talk.'

'Got nowt to talk about.'

'It's "nothing", Danny, not "nowt",' said me Aunty Tina. Geordie wasn't allowed in her house.

'Football,' said me mam. 'Talk to your cousins about that. You could speak for months about football.'

But Tabitha was too little, and Marcus was into tennis. So I just went sulky instead.

After lunch while some of the grown-ups got stuck into the booze, me, Tabitha, Marcus, Gran and Granda sat on the sofa and watched a James Bond film. Gran had forgotten to put her hearing aid in, and we had to watch the film at full volume. Was that loud I thought it would shatter the patio windows.

After James Bond had saved the world I went for a wander. Found me mam and Callum in the kitchen. Could tell straightaway he was in a mood. Didn't have to look at him, just needed to look at her.

'I don't want you to drive,' said me mam, arms folded.

'I've not had mush.'

'You've been drinking since you got here.'

They both spotted me, watching.

'Your mum and I are just having a bit of a disagreement, General. What she doesn't seem to realise is that I'm the driver in the house.'

'Not when you've been drinking,' said me mam.

Callum was swaying like he was on a train with nothing to hold on to.

'I know my limit, girl,' he said, pointing one of his fat fingers at her.

'Drink driving's bad,' I said.

Callum's face screwed up like he was stopping a sneeze, and he turned his little eyes on me. 'This has got nothing to do with you, General.'

'But I'm in the car as well.'

'Just stay out of it, Danny, please,' said me mam.

'Don't worry, General, you've seen I'm a bloody good driver,' said Callum, putting an arm around me shoulder. 'Couple of drinks isn't going to change that.'

Either Aunty Tina had super-human hearing or the walls in her house were as thin as bog paper, 'cos she turned up at the door and knew exactly what was going on.

'You can leave the car here, Callum,' she said, all rosy-cheeked from the fire, and too much wine.

'Nice of you to offer, but we're going, and I'm driving, and that, is end of story.'

'We could ring for a taxi,' said Aunty Tina.

'Do you not understand the meaning of "end of story"?' went Callum.

'I do not want Kim and Danny's lives put at risk,' said Aunty Tina. 'Not for the sake of a few pounds.'

'Have you any idea how much taxis cost on Christmas Day?' said Callum, with a laugh to show he thought she was an idiot.

'I don't care. I'll pay.'

'I've had enough of this,' muttered Callum. 'We're going.'

Me mam and Aunty Tina went into the laundry room to talk, while Callum went to grab the coats.

They were in the laundry room for ages.

Callum bashed on the door. 'It's a long walk back to Whickham,' he shouted.

Me mam appeared, looking upset. Aunty Tina never came out at all.

'Nice to see you,' said Callum, sticking his head into the front room, where everyone was sitting around, too full to move.

Me mam and me gave everyone super-quick hugs and kisses, got in Callum's car, and roared off, gravel flying.

Simply having a wonderful Christmas time.

Don't think the gadgie on the radio would be singing that if he was in our car. The atmosphere was like you get in the playground just before two lads are about to have a scrap.

'Slow down,' said me mam.

But he ignored her, like he always does, and drove, like he always drives, mad fast, like police cars don't exist. Saw his face in the mirror. Callum had red teeth to go with his red face. Looked like a vampire, after more blood. Mam just gripped her seat, her knuckles snow-white.

When we got back I asked if I could watch telly, but Callum shouted at me to go and play football in the back garden instead. Was freezing outside, but I did as I was told. Turned the kitchen lights on and practised penalties into me new goal. But it's pointless when you've got no goalie, so I kicked the ball against the shed instead, as hard as I could.

Could hear him shouting at me mam, even from outside. I started shaking, and it wasn't just the cold. Couldn't think what me mam had done wrong. All she'd said was that he'd drunk too much to drive home. She was just trying to keep us alive.

It didn't feel like Christmas Day any more. It felt like Crappy Day. I hated it. I wanted to go back to Amy's, but they were having relatives round. I went behind the shed, sat on the ball and covered me ears with me hands.

Later on I felt a tap on me shoulder.

'What you doing here?' said me mam.

'Sitting on the ball.'

'I'll make your tea.'

We went inside. No sign of him. No sound from the giant telly. Callum had gone to the pub.

Mam was dead quiet as she turned the gas on.

'Y'alreet, Mam?'

She nodded.

'Why does Callum get so angry?'

Mam put her hand to her mouth to try to stop a cry coming out, but she didn't manage it.

'I don't know, son. I just don't know.'

Seven

•

Spring turned up, and I turned fourteen. A few days after that it was Callum's birthday. Didn't like sharing the same star sign as him, but nothing I could do about that.

He decided to have a party.

His brother, Ian, arrived with his wife and three kids. His brother was even fatter than Callum, but not so smiley. There was his sister, Louise, who was skinny and had a tattoo of a fish on her leg. She had a toddler with her, but her husband must have stayed behind. Then there was Callum's mam, who looked like she'd run a marathon, wheezing a lot, and sitting down all the time. There were a bunch of other people as well, but I forgot their names.

None of Callum's lot were from round here, but they were still friendly.

'So you work in a call centre, Kim,' said Ian, nursing a can of beer to his chest like a bairn. 'Nice accent, you Geordies. Just don't get me to try it. I sound like a drunken German.'

Everyone laughed.

Louise walked up and gave me mam a hug. 'This is Kim, is it? We've heard lots about you.'

'All good, I hope,' went me mam, looking a bit nervous.

'Yes, Callum said he's found a right diamond in you.'

Me mam grinned. Think she liked being called that.

'Callum can be very generous,' said me mam.

'Oh, yes, heart of gold, my brother. He'd do anything for anyone,' said Louise, as she watched Callum giving their mam a paper plate piled high with meat.

Everyone seemed to really like Callum. Maybe it was the beer that was doing it.

'I hear Callum calls you General?' said Louise, looking at me.

'Aye.'

'Aye, aye? Maybe he should have called you Captain?'

Not much of a joke. But we laughed anyway.

While the grown-ups drank and stuffed their faces, I went to play football with Scott, Ian's ten-year-old.

Was good to have someone to have a kick-about with. He was a decent player too. For a young lad.

A canny day all round.

The one weird thing about the party was that the only people there were Callum's lot. Not one of me mam's mates turned up. And none of our relatives. Maybe they were busy.

After that life went on as normal, or abnormal, depending on how you look at it. Me mam was still in love with Callum, I think. But she was different from when he first arrived. Wasn't so smiley, and didn't hear so much of her canny voice, like she'd run out of things to say. Needed to get talking lessons off me gran.

'Y'alreet, Mam?' I'd say.

'Yeah.'

Just, 'Yeah', not even, 'Thanks for asking, Danny, I'm fine, thank you very much.'

And I noticed me mam didn't go out as often. She used to go down the Quayside with her mates or spend the day with Gran or meet Aunty Tina for a coffee. Now she only goes out with Callum. Not sure why. I mean, I haven't dumped all me mates just because I'm seeing Amy.

Apart from falling in love with Callum, me mam had also fallen in love with drink. When it was just her and me, I hardly ever saw her with a glass in her hand. Now it wasn't just chocolate biscuits she was mad for.

Me mam was guzzling most nights. When Callum got home he poured her a big glass of wine. Sometimes she didn't even wait for him to come back. *Glug, glug* went the bottle. Not because it was a birthday or she'd got paid, just because it was Tuesday, or the rain had stopped.

But even when me mam had a drink on the go, Callum went out. To the pub, always the pub. I was nervous when he came back. Never quite knew what would come out of his mouth. Or what he'd do next.

Remember once hearing the front door go. Instead of staying downstairs with me mam, he came up to see me. Didn't want him in me room. Not that I could stop him. It was his house.

'Okay, General,' he said, breathing heavy, even though he'd just walked up the stairs.

I was on me bed, on me mam's laptop.

'What you watching?'

'YouTube.'

Hoped he'd be happy with me answer and leave. But he came in. I felt the bed sink as he sat down next to me. I could smell beer, and his sweat.

'We need to have a little chat.'

I wanted to shout for me mam. But what could she do?

'Apparently you've been asking your mum why I shout at her?'

Felt me hands go clammy. Was he going to scream at me? Was he going to hit me?

'I only do it 'cos I love her,' he said, his voice slurry. 'Do you understand that, General? I only ever want her to be happy. But she doesn't always understand me, and what I want.'

He moved closer to me. The bed sank even further, like a boat capsizing. Me heart was going like the clappers.

'We're gonna make a great team, General. I need you on my side. You'll be my top striker.'

He put his face close to mine. I closed my eyes. Thought he was going to kiss me. Instead he rubbed me hair.

'I give her so much, your mum. Like I give you so much. And I just want something back in return. A bit of obedience, a bit of respect, a bit of love. It's not too much to ask, is it?'

'Guess not.'

'I want you to tell me if she's speaking to people she shouldn't be speaking to. Going places she shouldn't. Planning things when my back's turned.'

'Like what?'

'Anything that threatens what we've got, General. Because I've given you all this,' he said, looking round like it was a palace, instead of a room with clothes all over the floor. 'We don't want anything to destroy that, do we?'

Looked back at YouTube.

'Do we?'

'S'pose not.'

'Definitely not. So if you see or hear your mum doing anything out of the ordinary, you make sure you tell me first, yeah?'

Could never say yes to that.

He grabbed me head with his hands and made me nod.

'That's better, Danny. Remember, we're a team, General. Us boys have got to stick together.'

He rubbed me hair one more time, got off me bed and left.

Didn't know what to make of what I'd just heard. Did he really want me to spy on me own mam? Why would he want to do that? She works for a call centre, not MI5.

After his little talk Callum would sometimes ask if me mam ever phoned anyone when he was out, or if anyone phoned her, or if she did anything different.

Always had the same answer. 'No idea. I was in me room.' I'd never snitch on me mam.

When summer came Callum booked a villa in Spain for us. It was great to be going on holiday. Me and me mam had never been away anywhere, not even Carlisle. For once it felt like we were a proper family, going away together and having a laugh, like all the other kids at school. I realised I was wrong to stash me head with bad thoughts about Callum. You've got to love someone to want to take them away on holiday, haven't you? And paying for me as well, when I'm not even his son. How good is that?

Going abroad was almost as exciting as being in the shed with Amy. We had our own villa with a pool, and I had a bedroom twice the size of the one back home, looking out over the mountains. But the best bit was the beach. Nothing like Whitley Bay. It's as if our sea gets filled from the cold tap, and this one gets filled from the hot tap. It was belter sticking your head underwater without coming up gasping, dying of hypothermia. Wish the Spanish Sea and the North Sea would swap.

Apart from Real Madrid and Barcelona, I didn't know much about Spain, but I found the Spanish eat the same food as us. They sold burgers, chicken, steak, pies, chips. It was just like being in Gateshead, except mad hot. Me mam and Callum seemed dead happy with the place. They'd lie by the pool and turn red, go to the bar, go for a snooze, then go get some scran. I'd swim, watch movies and send messages to Amy.

It was the first time I'd spent a lot of time with Callum and I could see why me mam still loved him. He'd flash the cash all day long. On the last day Callum said he was going to treat us to some local food. He found a posh place with tablecloths, that did rice and fish in a bowl the size of a dustbin lid. Didn't like the look of it, but it tasted lush. Callum and me mam drank way too much, and afterwards they both conked out by the side of the pool. Me mam woke up first and spotted Callum snoring away on his lounger. The drink had given her a mad idea.

'Are you sure, Mam?' I said, as I watched her unravel the hosepipe. But the drink had destroyed any common sense she had left.

She stuck the hosepipe down Callum's shorts and turned it on.

Water must have been freezing 'cos he shot miles in the air.

Laughed meself silly.

Me mam and Callum were both screaming as he chased her round the pool.

'Come here,' he shouted.

Me mam was laughing her head off as she slipped and slid around the pool. The drink had made her legs useless, but Callum wasn't much better, his belly swaying from side to side as he tried to catch her.

Was the funniest thing I'd seen in ages.

Me mam slipped on a wet patch and Callum finally caught her.

She was still laughing like mad.

Then the laughing stopped.

Callum's arm was round her neck, tight.

'Let go of me,' she said, her words coming out all strange.

But he didn't.

I could see he was hurting her.

'Let her go,' I screamed.

'Thought you Geordies were meant to be tough,' he said, his fat arm round her neck, squeezing hard.

I ran over to him and tried to grab his arm, but he was too quick. He pushed me in the chest with his free hand and I fell backwards into the pool.

Wasn't ready.

Swallowed water.

Came to the surface, gasping. Couldn't touch the bottom. Couldn't breathe. Me mam and me both choking, choking.

Through blurry eyes I could see him, his arm still around her neck, me mam on her knees. The only sound came from Callum. Heavy breaths as he squeezed, squeezed.

I got me breathing back, and swam as fast as I could to the steps. Had no idea how I'd stop him. I needed a weapon. Couldn't see anything sharp anywhere. Then I spotted it, a wine bottle, next to Callum's lounger. I'd smash it over his head. But before I got to the top of the steps I looked up and saw him loose his grip. Me mam fell to the ground, her face white, eyes staring, mouth sucking in whatever air it could find. Too shocked to get her cries out.

I felt sick. As if I was the one who'd been strangled.

He stood over her. Fists clenched. Like a boxer.

Then he looked at me.

'You don't let people get away with stuff. Ever.'

Eight

• •

Never normally look forward to getting back to school, but I did this year. School meant being away from home, away from him. There was another reason I was glad to be back – Amy, the one person who could take me mind off everything that had gone on.

She and her family had gone to Loch Lomond. Said they couldn't afford to go abroad this year. Saving to have a loft put in.

'How was Scotland?' I asked her.

'Grim. Rained a lot. And when it wasn't raining we had a plague of midgies. They got everywhere.'

'Lucky old midgies.'

Amy gave me a playful punch.

'And being stuck in a caravan for two weeks. It was like being in prison.'

'Thought you liked your family.'

'I do. But doesn't stop them getting on me nerves. If me dad suggests Scotland again next year I'm leaving home.' Amy took me hand. 'So where would you like to go on holiday with me?'

'Be happy with two weeks in your shed.'

Amy gave me a not-so-playful punch.

'How was Spain?'

Good question. Ninety-nine per cent of it was great, but that one per cent had destroyed all the other per cents. It had ruined everything.

'It was hot.'

'That pool you had looked amazing.'

Felt sick when she said that.

'Aye, but the sea was better. Like jumping in the bath. Except I wasn't naked.'

'That would be cruelty to fish.'

Then her face went from happy to worried in a flash.

'Hello, gorgeous,' said a voice.

I turned and saw Lanky Dave Barns. He'd joined at the end of Year Eight. When some lads start school they're that quiet you don't even realise they're there. Lanky Dave was not like that. Always gobbing off.

He was proper bad. On top of that, he was taller than half the teachers.

Amy angled her face away, ignoring him.

'You haven't replied to me texts,' said Lanky Dave.

'That's because I delete them the second they arrive.'

'What about that picture I sent you, eh?' he said, smirking.

'Deleted.'

For a minute it felt like being back at home. Something going on I didn't get, and me stuck in the middle.

'What's gannin on?' I said.

'On your bike, Croft,' said Lanky Dave.

Clenched me fists tight. I wanted to smash him in the face. But not sure I could reach that far.

'Just leave him alone,' said Amy.

Lanky Dave stared down at me. 'What's he got that I haven't got?'

'Me,' she said.

Laughed.

Don't think Lanky Dave liked being made fun of. But he wasn't smart enough to come up with anything better.

'I'll be in touch,' said Lanky Dave, giving Amy the eye.

He swaggered off down the street, spitting in people's gardens.

Gobsmacked.

'What was all that about, Amy?'

'Nothing.'

'Nothing? If that's nothing, I'd hate to see something.'

'He's just been sending me stuff.'

'How did he get your number?'

'Got it off Chloe. Grabbed her phone.'

'You don't seem that bothered.'

Amy shrugged. Just like someone else I know.

'And what's this picture he sent you?'

'Danny, it's nothing. I can handle this. I'll speak to Mr Hetherington if he oversteps the mark.'

'Seems like he has already.'

'Loads of lads at school send texts and stuff.'

'I don't want him sending you anything.'

'Just chill out.'

How are you meant to chill when your blood's boiling?

Amy gave me a little kiss on me hot face.

'Don't get yourself all worked up. It's going to be fine, Danny.'

Nine

• •

Now I had two people to worry about.

Couldn't figure out Amy's reaction to Lanky Dave. Did she think he was just going to disappear, or get bored with annoying her, or suddenly start fancying blokes? I mean me mam does nothing and guess what happens? Callum walks all over her like a pavement. I didn't want what was happening to me mam to happen to Amy.

Since we got back from Spain nothing has changed at home. Even though he nearly killed her, me mam goes on like it never happened. Like it was a dream. But every second of it is tattooed on me brain. Me mam must need glasses. Why can't she see what I can see? When he comes back from the pub he's not a bloke you want to share a room with. He swears more, shouts more, and gets angry at the slightest thing. But me mam just smiles, soaks it all up and makes his tea, like he's just pretending. Like he's off the telly.

It was starting to do me head in.

• • •

One night I woke up and heard a loud crash and shouting. Thought it might be burglars. Secretly hoped it was. Carl's house had got broken into two weeks ago. They got a TV, a microwave and a sofa. Must have had a van.

Crept downstairs and saw the front room light was on. I could hear quiet crying. Even though I've got no god, not like Amy, I pretended I did and made up a prayer. Please, God, let me mam be all right.

Turned the door handle. Callum must have spotted it.

'Go back upstairs, Danny,' he shouted.

Let go of the handle like it was red hot.

'Yeah, just go to bed, Danny,' said me mam softly.

Thought she must be all right if she can talk. Not like in Spain.

I wanted to go in, but I was scared of what Callum might do, so I went back to bed and crawled under the duvet. Just lay there listening to them. When I say them, I mean Callum. He made nearly all the noise. Every now and then I'd hear a quieter voice, me mam. She did about five per cent of the sound. Then he'd be off again. I felt sick inside. I hated it, but what could I do? Callum was too strong. The way he knocked me into that pool, like I was a paper cup.

I pulled the duvet over me head and eventually went to sleep.

Next morning I put on me school uniform and had a quick peek in the front room. It was normal, like nothing had happened. I went in the kitchen. Me mam was standing at the sink looking outside even though there was nothing to look at, just grass.

'Where's Callum?' I said.

'Gone to work.'

I had loads of questions, but there was one main question right at the front of the queue.

'What happened last night?'

Me mam turned round slow and stared at me. 'Nothing happened, Danny.'

'I'm not stupid, you know. I've got ears.'

'Danny, what goes on between me and Callum is our business.'

'So I'm just meant to roll over and go to sleep, am I, even when he's bashing you?'

'Danny, this is nothing to do with you.'

ME MAM. ME DAD. ME.

'What about Spain?' I shouted. 'Has that got nothing to do with me, an' all?'

'It was a mistake.'

Laughed. Couldn't stop it.

'You just put a hose down his shorts. No reason to go and *strangle* you.'

'I'm not talking about this, Danny.'

'What's that mark on your face?'

Me mam turned away to wash some plates in the sink. But she didn't roll her sleeves up. Just dunked them straight in the soapy water.

'Did he grab you by the arms?'

Silence.

Except for the squeak of soap on plates.

'Have you gone deaf like your mam?'

But she said nothing. Just carried on washing the dishes, even though her sleeves were getting sopping wet.

I'd had enough.

Went out and slammed the kitchen door. Then slammed the front door.

Thought that's how it's going to be. For the rest of me life.

Ten

• • •

The day the clocks went back. That's when it all changed.

I went up to me room to watch YouTube, but wasn't in the mood. Too many questions eating away at me brains. Why did he do it? And why wouldn't she stop him doing it? I sat staring at the screen. The silence was killing me. I needed answers.

I went to Google. The oblong box waiting for me question. What could I ask? Can someone out there save me mam? Anyone got a cure for Callum? What do you do when your mam won't listen to you? The internet's meant to have all the answers. Maybe I could find something to make sense of what was going on in me house.

I got me two fingers ready and started typing. *Tell me about women being hit at home*, I wrote. I sat staring at the words. Was there a better question to ask? Probably. But couldn't think of one. I was scared to know what the answer might be. But, like pushing open the kitchen door, I had to find out.

With a shaky finger I pressed 'Search'.

Battered. Bashed. Beaten. Biffed. Mullah'd. Twatted. Smacked. Punched. Kicked. Thumped. Hit. Smashed. Walloped. Lamped. Mugged. Stabbed. Burned. Bullied. Heard them all. But there was something I'd never heard before, till now.

Domestic violence.

I found a site with loads of stuff about women being hit. This is what it said.

Young women are most at risk. Me mam. She's not old. *Most women never report domestic violence to the police.* Me mam. *Women who suffer domestic abuse try to hide the fact that they've been hurt.* Me mam. *Women can become withdrawn and not talk to family or friends.* Me mam.

It was like whoever wrote this had been spying on her.

It got worse and worse. It said two women a week are killed by their partners.

Got a pen and paper and worked it out. Two times fifty-two. Holy hell. One hundred and four mams a year. It would be like all the women in our street and Belfry Close being murdered in one go.

The bad stuff went on and on. *One in four women will experience domestic violence in their lifetime. It has a greater chance of repeat victimisation than any other crime.* Think that means it just keeps on happening. Me mam has got to read this. Then she'll know what he's like, and that she has to get rid of him, before he does her in.

I put the laptop down and took a little walk round me room. I felt like I did the day Callum drove like a nutter along the Roman road. Scared and excited. Scared that what was happening to all those other mams was happening to me own mam. Excited that I'd found it in time.

I went back and read a bit more. Found stuff about the domestic abusers. *Perpetrators don't need alcohol to be violent.* Callum. Like the time he kicked that lass's car down the coast road. Hadn't even had a shandy. They don't like being disobeyed. Callum. The Christmas Day disaster. *They often try to keep their partner from family or friends.* Callum. Me mam never sees anyone any more. *They can encourage their partner to take drink and drugs.* Callum. Always forcing booze down me mam. Jealousy. Callum. Wanting to know if me mam was talking to anybody. The list was long. Most of it describing the bloke downstairs watching telly.

I'd had enough. Turned the laptop off. Was good

to know that me mam wasn't the only one. Was bad to know that she was just like all the others.

I needed me mam to read this, but not with him sitting there. I'd have to wait for the right moment. It came along the next night. Callum had gone to the pub. Me mam was on the sofa reading *Hello!* and eating chocolate biscuits. She'd put on even more make-up. Guess she didn't want anyone at work to know what had happened. Like it said on the website.

'Mam?'

She looked up.

'Been doing your homework?' she said, looking at the laptop.

'No, I've got something to show you.'

She put her magazine down and I placed the laptop on her lap. Mam looked at it and smiled. Then the smile went out quick, like a lightbulb.

'Read it,' I said.

Mam put the lid down and picked up her *Hello!*

'Mam.'

She just kept flipping through the pages, looking at all those celebs with their perfect lives and perfect faces that never get hit.

'Mam, read it. Please.'

She shook her head.

I was that frustrated I kicked the sofa. Her plate of biscuits flew all over the floor.

'Danny,' she moaned.

'Got your attention now, have I?'

She looked at me, blank-faced, like a shop-window dummy.

'I just want you to look at the website. I want you to read about what he's doing to you. It's there. Tons of it.'

Mam stared at the biscuits on the carpet, as if wondering how they got there.

'Do you want him to kill you? Is that what you want? He's mad enough.'

'I don't need to read it.'

'Why not? Have you become a world expert on it? Do you know what's going to happen?'

Me mam kept on staring, like Callum had kicked all the life out of her.

'I'm scared for you, Mam. The people who wrote the website aren't lying, are they? It was written by coppers. They're not allowed to lie. I don't want you to die.'

I thought me words were working on her. That she'd see sense.

Thought wrong.

'It's gonna be okay, Danny.'

Let out a scream.

'Maybe Callum's right about your backside. Go back to your biscuits.'

I stormed out of the room and slammed the door. Then I grabbed me ball, turned the kitchen lights on, and went in the back garden. Kicked the ball against the shed, dead hard, then I kicked the shed, even harder. Made a massive hole in it, but I couldn't give a monkey's. It was Callum's shed, he could mend it.

Two women killed every week.

All those mams.

Screamed again.

But it wasn't just Callum I was mad with. It was me mam.

Why wouldn't she read the website? Why wouldn't she believe me? Why wouldn't she do something about it? Why wouldn't she leave him? Why?

Eleven

•

Me mind went round and round like a waltzer at the Hoppings.

Me mam was never going to do anything to save herself. Like she had a death wish. All I could think about was killing Callum. But how? Poison him? Problem is, I can't cook. He'd know I was up to something if I gave him a plate of dodgy-looking scran. Push him in front of a train? But Callum went to work in his car. Stab him? He'd get the knife off me with his quick fingers before I got close to that fat belly.

Didn't have a clue what to do, so I spoke to Barry. He knows tons of stuff. 'Do your mam and dad fight?'

'All the time, man,' he said. 'There's a constant battle for the TV remote.' Barry put on voices like he was his mam and dad. Deep voice: 'I'm watching the football.' High voice: 'You're always watching football.' Deep voice: 'You're always watching cooking.' High voice: 'At least cooking's good for you. You can't eat a football.' Deep voice: 'What do you mean? That Yorkshire pudding you made tasted just like leather.'

Laughed.

'But do they ever fight, you know, proper fight?' I said, raising me fists.

Barry shook his head. 'Na. The only time I've seen them fight was last summer when me dad filled a water pistol up with cold water and squirted it down me mam's top when she was sunbathing in the back garden. They had a right ding-dong over the pistol. Both ended up in the paddling pool.'

Felt sick when Barry mentioned that.

'Does your dad ever get drunk?' I said.

'Aye. Every Friday.'

'And what does he do?'

'Falls asleep.' Barry did a loud snore like a pig with a microphone. 'Crashes on the sofa. He's too heavy to carry upstairs, so we leave him. Sometimes he's still there in the morning.'

Thought of a different question.

'What would you do if some bloke bashed your mam?'

Barry scratched his chin, which had just started to get hairs. 'I'd tell me dad, and he'd beat him to a pulp.' Barry looked at me weird. 'Anyway, why all the questions?'

'Just writing a story for English, about a bloke who does that sort of thing.'

I thought of asking Amy, but she'd only come back with loads of questions, and I'd end up answering them. Didn't want her to know what went on in our house. I asked Andrea Watson instead. She's the brainiest lass in our year. Makes us all look totally daft. I plucked up the courage to ask her at break time.

'Andrea?'

'Yes, Danny.'

'This is just a hypogenic question.'

'I think you mean hypothetical.'

'Yeah, probably.' I could already feel me face changing colour. 'What would you do if someone, not your dad, hurt your mam?'

Andrea put her thinking face on. 'I'd call the police.'

'Other than the police.'

Andrea rolled her eyes.

'My mother and father are separated, but I'd probably call my father.'

'Oh.'

'Why do you ask?' said Andrea, suddenly all serious. 'Is everything okay with your mother?'

'Everything's fine,' I said, walking away.

'Are you sure, Danny?' she shouted.

'Aye. Thanks, Andrea.'

I asked a few more kids.

'What would I do if a bloke bashed me mam?' said Carl, scratching his head. 'I'd ring me dad. He'd smash their face in.'

'Oh.'

'If someone bashed me mam?' said Ben. 'I'd call for me dad. He'd get a tank and blow him up. Then he'd destroy him with a flame-thrower. Then he'd shoot him.'

Ben's got quite a vivid imagination.

Apart from Gavin, who said the SAS, and Tony, who said his mam was dead, everyone came up with the same answer – their dad.

If I was going to get rid of Callum, I was going to have to ask me dad. There was just one problem. I had no idea who me dad was.

Twelve

• •

'Danny, I hear you've been talking to Andrea.'

Should have known this would get to Amy. Lasses love talking. It's their number one hobby.

'Aye.'

'Why didn't you ask me?'

'Andrea was closer.'

Amy laughed, for one second.

'Is your mam having trouble with Callum?'

'Not really.'

'What sort of answer's that?' she said, folding her arms tight.

'They have the occasional shouting match.'

Though it wasn't much of a match when Callum was involved. Ten – nil, to him.

'But you weren't talking about shouting. You were asking her about mams getting beaten up?'

What is it with lasses and their questions?

'So what's been happening with you and Lanky Dave?'

'Stop changing the subject. We're talking about your mam.'

'Can we talk about something else, Amy? I hear Newcastle are after a new number nine.'

'I'm being serious, Danny. You used to talk a lot about your mam and Callum.'

'Nowt to talk about.'

'And you don't invite me round your place any more.'

'It's a long way up Whickham Bank.'

Part of me wanted to tell Amy. Wanted to tell her everything. But the other part, the part that always wins, had parked a boulder in front of me mouth. It was saying, 'No, bad idea, Danny. She can't help you. You'll scare her away. It's for you to fix.'

'If we're going out I don't want us to have any secrets,' said Amy.

'Like you not telling me anything about Lanky Dave.'

Amy's face told me I'd got her on that one.

'I'm concerned, that's all, Danny. If something happened you'd tell me, wouldn't you? Wouldn't you?'

Did the world's smallest nod.

'Can I have a proper answer, please?'

'Yes, Amy. I'd tell you.'

Thirteen

• • •

'**Mam, can you** tell me about me dad?'

'I've told you a million times, Danny.' Exaggeration. 'I'm not talking about him.'

'I just want to know who he is, that's all. All the other kids know who their dads are, even the ones who've copped off with someone. Why won't you tell me?'

The question usually ended with me mam slobbing on a chair, or blowing out air or staring out of the window, sometimes all three. And that's what happened this time.

'Some things are best left in the past, Danny.'

'Why? Was he bad?' I nearly said, 'like Callum'. Didn't. Should have.

'Yeah, he was bad, in his own way.'

'Which way?'

'His way.'

'How bad?'

'Just bad,' she snapped.

Bad was what I needed, a really bad dad to do something to Callum and make him stop.

'Was he a criminal?'

'Danny, I said I don't want to talk about him and now you've gone and made me talk about him.'

'Do you not know where he lives then?'

'Yes I do, but I've got no intention of telling you.'

Tried one last thing.

'But if I've got a dad, why can't I see him? All the other kids see theirs.'

This had just the right effect on me mam. She got up from the sofa, came over and gave me a big cuddle.

'Danny, your dad and I went our separate ways even before you were born. We had our reasons, and please don't ask me what they were.' I was just about to do that. 'It's best if we leave things the way they are.'

'Just you, me and Callum?'

'Yes, just you, me and Callum,' she said, trying hard to smile.

Me dad must have done something really bad if this

was better than that. I realised that me mam was never going to tell me about me dad, not in a trillion years. But if she wouldn't, I knew someone who would.

'Hi, Gran.'

'Eeh, hello, Danny, haven't seen you in ages,' said me gran, looking me up and down. 'Was gonna say you've grown, but I'm not sure you have.'

Gave her a massive hug.

'What brings you here?'

'Me bike.'

'What's that?'

'Me bike,' I shouted.

'Oh.'

'Have you not got your hearing aid in, Gran?' I said, at full volume.

'Na, I divvent like them. Hurt me lugs.'

Me gran would rather be half-deaf than have sore ears. Maybe she thinks we all talk rubbish.

'Where's your mam?'

'Home.'

'Haven't seen her in donkeys.' Even more wrinkles filled her forehead. 'Is she okay, Danny?'

'Think so.'

'And what's Callum up to?'

'The usual.'

'Chatterbox, aren't you? Howay inside.'

We went in. The house smelled just the way I

remembered it, like a flower shop. Looked at the stairs I used to slide down on me coat. Saw pictures of me mam and me on the wall. It was good to be back.

I followed her into the front room.

'Sit there, Danny, so you're on me good side.'

Flopped down next to her on the sofa. Gran's house was dead clean, with lots of stuff in glass cabinets, like a museum. Granda was sitting in the corner, staring at nothing.

'Y'alreet, Granda?'

Didn't even turn his head.

Gran smiled as if to say, *Don't bother, son.*

'Would you like a glass of pop, Danny?' she said. 'You always used to love pop.'

'Aye—' nearly forgot – 'please.'

She went and got me a glass of lemonade. Tasted good. Felt a burp building, but managed to keep it to meself. Even me gran's ears could hear one of me monster belches.

'So how come you've decided to pay us a visit?'

'Want to know where me dad is.'

Gran didn't have much colour in her face, but what she did have went and left. She looked a bit like the lass whose car got kicked by Callum on the coast road. Gran took in some quick gulps of air like she was sinking underwater. This made her cheeks go back to pink again.

She put her spotty hand on mine. 'What's brought this on, Danny?' she said, looking worried.

'Nothing's brought it on, Gran. Just want to know where he is.'

'Have you asked your mam?'

'Aye, she'll tell me nowt.'

Gran looked at me over the top of her glasses. 'If she won't, I don't think I can.'

'Why not?'

'Because your mam must have a very good reason.'

'What reason?'

Gran scratched her chin. She had little hairs, just like Barry.

'There's things in life you don't need to know about, Danny. Maybe one day you'll get to hear all about him. But now's not that time.'

'What about in five minutes?'

'No, not in five minutes either. In a few years.'

'I don't want to wait for years.'

'Well, you'll just have to. You've got to be patient.'

Then she put her hand on mine again.

'Tell your mam to call me.'

'That's if he lets her,' I muttered.

'What's that, son?'

'Nothing, Gran. Nothing.'

Fourteen

•

I sometimes went round Amy's house after school. Liked going there. There was a good feeling to the place. It felt safe. Like nothing was ever going to kick off. Probably scared to do anything in front of Jesus, who was watching them from crosses, all over the house.

But I remember one time her mam and dad actually had a bit of a barney.

'I'm going out tonight, Mark,' said Amy's mam. 'It's been in the diary for ages.'

'I was going to watch the match at the pub,' he said, his voice all disappointed.

'You can watch it here.'

'Not the same.'

'It's a game on a telly. Don't tell me it's a different match at the pub.'

'It's the atmosphere.'

I'd come to realise that adults can argue about absolutely anything. Amy and me sat listening to them in the front room.

'What'll happen now?' I asked Amy.

'Me dad'll stop in and watch the football.'

'He'll let your mam win?'

Amy looked at me, with her quizzing face. 'Do you mean Callum always wins in your house?'

'Well, he's the bloke, isn't he?'

'What planet are you on, Danny? Have you not heard of equality?'

Heard of it. Just not sure I'd seen any of it. Couldn't think of a single time when me mam had got her own way. Whatever Callum said was the law.

'It's just not how things go in our house.'

'That's sad,' said Amy, and she squeezed me hand.

Sure enough her dad agreed to stay in and watch the match. Then a few seconds later they were hugging in the hallway. No hard feelings.

Seeing what went on in Amy's house made me more determined than ever to find me dad. This was the sort of house I wanted to live in. One where little arguments didn't turn into enormous arguments. One where no one ever got hit.

I decided to go and see me Aunty Tina. She and me mam used to hang around together a lot. They can't have just talked about clothes all the time. Must have saved some room for family. Thought there was a chance she'd know something about me dad.

I told me mam I was going to see Amy.

It was way too far to cycle to Aunty Tina's so I got the bus, two buses, in fact. Took ages. Not like at Christmas, when we got there in about ten seconds.

Walked up the long drive to her house and rang the bell.

Door opened.

'Hello, Danny. My, this is most unexpected,' said Aunty Tina. I hadn't been round her house since Christmas.

'Hello, Aunty Tina.'

'Where's your mum?' she went, peering up the drive.

'At home with—' Even his name made me want to spit – 'Callum.'

'Has anything happened?' she said, with a worried look.

It would take all day to tell her what had gone on. But I wasn't going to. She wasn't the one to tell.

Shook me head.

She looked at me through slitty eyes. 'Are you sure everything's okay, Danny? I've spoken to your mum, but she doesn't seem herself. She hasn't been round here in ages.'

'You haven't been round our place in ages.'

Aunty Tina suddenly looked guilty, her fingers fidgeting with each other. 'Yes, well, after the way Callum went on, Greg doesn't want… doesn't want to go there. I've tried to meet her for a coffee, but she's always busy.'

'Yeah, busy.'

Busy didn't do it for Aunty Tina.

'Are you one hundred per cent sure everything's all right?'

No, Aunty Tina, everything is not all right. But don't you worry. I'm going to sort it.

'Aye, it's all right.'

'It's "yes", not "aye", Danny.'

'Yes, Aunty Tina.'

Her face lost its worried look.

'Your Uncle Greg has taken Tabitha and Marcus to tennis.'

'Haven't come to see them, I've come to see you.'

Her big brown eyebrows went up. 'Me?'

'Yes, you.'

'You'd better come in then.'

Kicked me trainers off at the door. Aunty Tina's house was even cleaner than Callum's and Gran's. Shoes weren't allowed in. Like they'd done something wrong.

We went into her front room. Took me jacket off and put it on a chair.

'Would you like a glass of something?'

'Yes, something.'

Stupid thing to say, but your head doesn't work proper when you're nervous.

Aunty Tina came back with a glass of orange juice. Tasted a bit weird.

Had bits in it.

'Well, this is a surprise,' she said, making a squeak with her bum when she sat on the leather sofa. Be even more of a surprise when she heard what I was after. 'So why have you come all this way?'

Took a glug of juice and choked on the stupid bits. Aunty Tina patted me back till the cough stopped.

'I've got a question for you.'

Aunty Tina leaned forwards. 'I'm all ears.'

'I want to know where me dad is.'

Aunty Tina sat back, arms folded. Didn't look so pleased to see me any more.

There was a long silence while she worked out what to say next.

'Where's this come from?'

'Me.'

'I know it's from you, Danny,' sighed Aunty Tina. 'I want to know why you're asking the question.'

'I'll be fifteen next March. Thought it was about time I knew who me dad was. Is.'

'I'm afraid I can't tell you,' she said, fiddling with the beads round her neck.

'Why not?'

'It's for your mum to tell you. Have you asked her?'

'Loads of times. She won't tell me. Where is he?'

Aunty Tina looked like one of those people on a quiz show who hasn't got a clue what the answer is. They'd love the money, they'd really love it, but they just haven't got a clue.

'Danny, are you sure everything's okay at home?'

Now it was like one of those cop programmes, when they ask the same question over and over.

'Yes,' I said, probably a bit too loud, and a bit too quick.

'It's just, after what happened here...' Didn't need reminding of that. 'You'd tell me if something was up, wouldn't you, Danny. You'd tell me?'

''Course I would. But I want to find me dad.'

Aunty Tina shuffled like she had an itch. 'It's a very complex situation we're talking about here.'

'But we're not talking about it.'

She got up and walked slowly around the room, still fiddling with her beads.

'Oh, Danny, Danny, Danny.'

Something told me that she wanted to tell me. I decided to help her. 'Just tell me a bit.'

Aunty Tina smiled. She had dead white teeth, like you see in adverts.

'You can't just know a bit, Danny.'

'Tell me everything then.'

She shook her head, and her beads jiggled. This was starting to do me brain in. I know grown-ups keep stuff from kids, but this was ridiculous. All I wanted was to find out where me dad is. Not too much to ask, is it?

'Is he dead?'

'No, Danny, he's not dead.'

'Is he in prison?'

She shook her head.

'But he's bad?'

'He was once.'

That'll do me.

'So why can't I see him?'

Aunty Tina scratched her cheek with four red finger-nails. 'You just can't, Danny, not without your mum's permission. I can't give you that.'

I stood up. I wanted to kick her stupid sofa, and all the knick-knacks on her shelves. Another house where everything was perfect.

'I want to see him,' I shouted.

'Calm down, Danny.'

'You don't understand.'

Aunty Tina came over and took me hand. I took it back. It's my hand. Not hers.

'What don't I understand? What are you talking about, Danny? Why are you so desperate to find him?'

The room fell silent, apart from a clock ticking on the mantelpiece, and Aunty Tina's breathing.

'Then can I write to him?'

'What?'

'Write to him. Don't need to see him, I can just write.'

'No, Danny. I can't, really I can't.'

'Well, I'm off then.'

Picked me jacket up and walked towards the door.

'What are you doing?' said Aunty Tina, her voice all shaky.

'Going home.'

'You can stay a bit longer if you like. I've made some carrot cake.'

'I want me dad. Not cake.'

Aunty Tina looked like I felt. Hopeless.

She followed me into the hall, and tried to help me put me coat on, but I grabbed it off her and did it meself.

'Do you want me to drive you home, Danny?'

'No.'

'I wish I knew what this was all about.'

Wish on, Aunty Tina.

I normally give her a hug, but not today. Didn't deserve it.

She looked at me, confused, then wrapped her arms round me. I wanted to break free, but didn't. Couldn't. I just felt weak, like all the muscles in me body had been removed. Hugs from me gran. Now from me aunty. Never thought I'd miss them. But I did. It reminded me of the times when we lived with me gran and granda.

Everyone there. Everyone happy. I felt safe. I knew this feeling wouldn't last, though. Aunty Tina would have things to do.

I saw a picture on the wall. It was Aunty Tina, Uncle Greg, Tabitha and Marcus, bunched up together on a beach, with proper smiles, not Callum ones. Me mam used to have pictures of us in our flat. But there's none where we live now. Just photos of racing cars. Like we don't exist.

The picture and the warm hug were too much. I started to cry. I'm not a cry-baby, really I'm not, but I couldn't stop them. The tears just kept coming.

'Oh, Danny,' she went.

Aunty Tina squeezed even more tears out of me. I felt stupid, sobbing over her nice hall carpet. She finally let go and went to get some tissues. I caught me face in the mirror. It didn't look like me, eyes red like a zombie, hair messed from the squeezing, face sad from the smiley picture.

Aunty Tina came back with a pile of tissues for me. I blew me nose, and reached for the front door handle. But before I got it she put her hand on mine.

'Wait.'

She hurried off into another room. Probably getting more tissues. A minute later she came back with a piece of paper in her hand. Too small to blow me nose on that. She stood there looking at it, like she didn't know why she'd got it. Then she shoved the paper in me palm, and put both her hands over mine, like jaws.

'When you write to him, tell him not breathe a word about who told you.'

'Yes, Aunty Tina.'

'And get your mum to call me. Please.'

'Yes, Aunty Tina.'

'And whatever you do, Danny, you must never tell your mum I gave this to you. Do you understand?'

I looked at her hands on mine.

'Do you understand?'

'Yes, Aunty Tina, I understand.'

Fifteen

• • •

I ran like a winger all the way down the street, with a grin as wide as the Tyne.

I knew what Aunty Tina had given me, even without looking. She'd given me me dad's address.

Stopped running when I reached the bus stop. I had that feeling you get on Christmas morning when you've got a present in your hands. You want to open it, you really do, but part of you doesn't want to open it, ever. You just want the excitement too much. That's what it was like with me bit of paper. But you can't stand it, you've got to know. I closed me eyes, counted to ten, then opened it.

Steve River, 9 Redward Gardens, Newington, Edinburgh.

Edinburgh? That's miles away. I thought me dad would live round here or down Durham way. What did he have to go and live in Scotland for? I needed him here.

Got the bus to Eldon Square, then another one to Gateshead, staring at the paper all the way home, thinking, thinking, thinking.

Walked in the back door.

'Where've you been?'

Me mam was doing something at the sink. The way mams do.

'Told you, Amy's.'

'You've been a long time.'

'So?'

Threw me coat on the floor.

'Hook.'

Put me coat on the hook.

Went in the front room. Callum was sitting in his usual chair watching cars go round and round. I'm sick of saying his name. From now on in me head I'm going to call him FB for Fat Bastard. I looked over at FB and smiled. For the first time since we came here I felt I had power over him. He might be bigger than me, might have more money than me, might have faster fingers than me, but from now on I knew I could beat him, because I had something in me pocket that could put a stop to him forever. I had the address of the bloke who was going to kill him.

But before I could get rid of FB, I had one small problem to solve, how to get to Edinburgh. I took the laptop into FB's office, opened it up, and tapped in the search box with me two fingers.

Where is Edinbru?

Do you mean: Edinburgh?

Yes, Mr Picky. Clicked. Loads of sites popped up. Edinburgh is the capital of Scotland. Knew that. Then something I didn't know. Edinburgh is a hundred and four miles from Newcastle. How the heck was I going to get all the way up there? Suppose I could ask me mam if we could go on a day trip, but if Aunty Tina knew me dad lived in Edinburgh, me mam would too.

'What do you want to go to Edinburgh for, Danny?' she'd ask with squinty eyes.

'To see the men in skirts.'

She'd know I was lying. Then she'd make me tell her why we were really going, then she'd lock me in me room, and I'd never get to see me dad and ask him for help, and FB would be off the hook, and me power would be gone, and me mam would keep getting battered. Until she was dead.

I clicked off the Edinburgh sites and deleted it in 'History'. Didn't want to leave a trail. That's how you get caught. I went back in the front room and sat on the sofa. The ideas in me head were going round and round, *meeee-ow*, *meeee-ow*, *meeeee-ow*, just like those stupid cars on the telly, getting nowhere.

I thought of writing me dad a letter, like Aunty Tina thought I was going to do.

> Dear Steve,
>
> You don't know me, but I'm Danny, your son. I realise we've never ~~talk~~ spoken, but could you do me a small favour? Could you kill me mam's boyfriend, please?
>
> Lots of love, Danny

How daft would that be? He'd think I was some sort of nutter. I needed to go and see him, tell him the whole story.

When the Formula One finished FB went to the pub, and Mam made me tea. I sat at the kitchen table staring at a fridge magnet of a Highland cow that Amy gave me.

'What's up?' she asked.

Mams are like detectives. They can spot things normal people can't.

I said nothing, which, as far as me mam was concerned, was like something.

'He's not a bad person, Danny,' she said. I tried not to

laugh at that, but a little pig snort escaped. 'We've just had a couple of bust-ups. Anyway, everyone sorts out their problems differently.'

She was right there. Me mam and FB could sort it out their way, I was going to sort it out mine. Before I could solve me problem, something happened, something so horrible I can hardly tell you, but I will.

A few days later it was me mam's birthday. She was thirty. I got her a box of chocolates. She seemed happy enough with it, even though it would screw up her diet. Me mam never stops thinking about her weight. FB sees to that.

FB bought her a big card with roses and sparkly bits on the front. I read the inside and nearly puked.

> YOU ARE THE SWEETEST WOMAN
> I HAVE EVER MET. MY LIFE WOULD
> BE EMPTY WITHOUT YOU.
> ALL MY LOVE, CALLUM. THIRTY KISSES

It didn't stop there. He also bought her a big saggy handbag, some flowers, some earrings, and a coat. A coat? What did she need another one of them for? She's got three. Anyway, that's what he gave her, and Mam seemed dead happy with it all. She kissed him, with her mouth open, like me and Amy do when no one's watching.

That night they went out for a meal somewhere posh. Must have been posh, 'cos FB put a tie on and me mam wore the shoes that make her feet hurt. I wanted to go to Amy's, but me mam said I couldn't 'cos it was a school night, so I stayed in and played games on the laptop.

Got some of me worst-ever scores. Couldn't concentrate for thinking about me mam.

Two women killed every week.

Wanted to know why people like me mam let people like Callum get away with murder.

Typed: *Why don't women run away from domestic violence?*

Yeah, explain that one Mr Google. Came up with a ton of reasons. One, they think he might hurt them even more. Two, they may be financially dependent. Three, they've got no self-esteem left. Four, they may feel ashamed of what's happened and think it's their fault. Five, they hope that the person will change. Six, they look back to the start of the relationship and hope that the good times will come back. Didn't know which ones were me mam. Had to be some of them. Maybe all of them.

Clicked off the site and deleted it in 'History'. Lay back on me bed, staring at the ceiling. They'd be in a restaurant now, eating, drinking, laughing, like nothing was wrong. But I knew different. Everything was wrong. Me mam had to get away from him. She just had to.

Took me clothes off, and crawled into bed.

'Happy birthday, Mam.'

Can't remember when they got back, forgot to look at the clock, but instead of going to bed me mam came in me room and woke me up. *Shake, shake, shake.* Freaked out when I saw her standing over me. Thought he must have hit her again. But Mam wasn't bashed, she was happy, and smelled like FB does when he's been to the pub.

'What is it, Mam?'

She had a grin FB would have been proud of.

'I've got some news for you Danny. Me and Callum are going to get married.'

Sixteen

•

How could she do it? How could she marry a bloke like FB? Me mam was officially mad.

I tried to close me eyes, but every time I did I saw her face again, all grinny, red teeth, and that mouth saying those words – *we're going to get married*. I got on me knees and punched the pillow as hard as I could again and again and again. Me mam was going to marry the bloke that batters her. The bloke that's going to kill her. Why doesn't she just throw herself off the Tyne Bridge?

I lay in bed listening to them, not rowing or fighting, just laughing like little bairns. I heard a bottle pop and a can *fsshhed*. They were still drinking, even though they'd already been drinking, even though they both had work in the morning. Drink does that to you. Makes you go daft.

He'd tricked her, that's what he'd done, with the card and the flowers and the earrings and the coat and the droopy bag. She thought he loved her, because he gave her tons of stuff. But she'd already forgotten about the other stuff he'd given her, the bruises, the black eye, the punch in the mouth, the headlock, the ear-bashings. It was like coats and bags counted for more.

I was that mad I screamed, like a total nutter. But they didn't hear me. They'd put the music on. They were having a party, just the two of them. I'd almost given up on getting to Edinburgh, but not any more. I couldn't let her marry him. That would mean he'd be around forever. She'd never get away. I didn't want him as me dad. I wanted me own dad, me real dad.

Next day I went to school and got shouted at.

'Danny,' shouted Mr Hetherington. 'I want to see your head on your shoulders, not on your desk.'

Laughs from every direction.

'See me after class.'

'Yes, Mr Hetherington.'

After the lesson everyone trooped out. Geoff Loosy drew a line across his throat, Mark Waters hummed the funeral march, and Lanky Dave said, 'You're dead, pal.' But Amy gave me arm a squeeze when she walked past and mouthed, 'Love you.' Her two little words made me insides squidge up.

Mr Hetherington sat behind his desk, arms folded, pocket full of pens.

'Is everything okay, Danny?'

'Yeah, everything's fine, sir.'

Didn't need to tell him. None of his business.

'Are you getting enough sleep?'

'Try to.'

'Then try a bit harder, will you?' he said, smiling.

Nodded.

'Now off you go.'

Ran to the door.

'And, Danny?'

Stopped.

'If there's anything wrong, you'd tell me?'

'Yes, Mr Hetherington.'

Thought that was the worst thing that would happen that day, but it wasn't even close. Something else won the gold medal for worst thing.

At break time Lanky Dave came up to me.

'You still seeing my lass.'

'Amy is not your lass,' I said, trying to keep me voice big.

Lanky Dave then put his face about a millimetre from mine. 'She's gagging for me. Like they all are.'

Loads of girls used to hang around Lanky Dave.

Reckoned the only reason he wanted Amy was because she wanted nothing to do with him.

'She'll come running to me soon enough,' he said, and he walked off, smirking.

I was mad with Lanky Dave for what he'd said. The mad came out of me after break. I was going up the stairs when he went past and dug an elbow in me ribs. I don't normally go mental, not even during a match when someone trips me when I'm clean through, but I went mental now. I jumped up, grabbed him round the neck and pulled him backwards.

Luckily, we weren't at the top of the stairs. Lanky Dave lost his balance and fell backwards, like a tree that had been chopped. I thought the kids further down might stop him. But they didn't. They just leaped out of the way, and he went right to the bottom.

Wazzocks.

Lanky Dave smacked his head on the ground and lay still. A pool of blood started to creep out of his thick, curly hair. A crowd stood round looking at it.

'What did you do that for, man?' said somebody.

'Divvent knaa,' I said back.

Teachers were there dead quick, like superheroes. Two of them carried Lanky Dave off. Mr Tobin, the PE teacher, stood at the bottom, his hairy arms crossed tight, his face molten angry.

'What happened?' he shouted.

'Croft pushed Barns down the stairs, sir,' said a voice from the crowd.

Could have tried to lie, but me face was covered in guilt.

'Come with me, Croft.'

Got taken to see Mrs Brighton, the head teacher. They kept me waiting outside her office for ages while they got the evidence. Then I got called in. Mrs Brighton's office looked more like a library than an office. Everywhere you looked were books. Mrs Brighton was a little woman with a big head. She sat behind her desk, staring at me over the top of her glasses.

'Sit down, Danny,' she said.

Parked meself on a chair in front of her desk.

'I want to know exactly what happened.'

'Dave Barns elbowed me, Mrs Brighton.'

'So you decided to throw him down the stairs?'

'I didn't think he'd fall. Not that far.'

She looked down at her notes. 'In the two and a bit years you've been with us you've had a good disciplinary record, Danny.' Not like some kids. Jimmy Archer in Year Ten set fire to the science lab. Got expelled. 'Is everything okay at home?'

She must have talked to Mr Hetherington.

'Yes, Mrs Brighton.'

She put her elbows on her desk and laced her fingers like she was saying her prayers.

'I don't want to see a repeat performance of this, do you hear me?'

'Yes, Mrs Brighton.' Or should that be, 'No, Mrs Brighton'?

'I've had to send David home. I abhor violence. I really don't want this sort of thing going on in my school, do you understand?'

'Sorry, Mrs Brighton.'

'I want you to write a note to David, apologising for what you did.'

'Yes, Mrs Brighton.'

I was starting to sound like a parrot.

'This will go on your record.' She looked at the door. 'You can go now, Danny.'

'Thanks, Mrs Brighton.'

I ran back to class.

Some of the lads thought it was great and patted me on the back like I'd won something, while the lasses looked at me with that disappointed face they're so good at. I told Amy the full story when I got the chance. She said I was amazing and gave me a mad snog behind church after school.

I thought that was the end of it, but it was just the start.

'Danny,' screamed me mam from the front room when I got home. 'I want a word.'

She was on the sofa with the laptop on her knees.

'What in God's name's been going on?'

The school must have sent her an email.

'Got into a bit of trouble, Mam.'

'Mrs Brighton said you pushed a boy down the stairs. He needed stitches.'

I kicked the skirting board with me heel.

'Don't do that, you'll mark it.'

Kicked it again.

'He said something bad about Amy. Then he elbowed me on the stairs.'

'Revenge never solved anything, Danny.'

'Really?'

'Yes, really.'

'Can you not remember what Callum said in Spain?'

Me mam bent forwards, a pained look on her face, as though the memory had torn through her, like a knife.

'You don't let people get away with stuff. Ever.'

Seventeen

• • •

Just when I thought I was never going to solve the Edinburgh problem, Amy came to the rescue.

'Are you going on the school trip, Danny?' she said, as we walked down the street after school.

'What school trip?'

'The one on the school email you clearly never read. We're going to be away for six whole days.' She grinned at me. 'And that means six whole nights.'

The thought of going away with Amy brought me out in goose bumps. Make that goose mountains. We'd never been away anywhere proper. Six days away with her would have been belter. But much as I wanted to go,

I still had a problem that needed solving, and Amy had just solved it.

'Mam?'

'What?' she said, as she lay on the sofa with a cup of smelly tea on her belly, and a pile of chocolate biscuits next to her. Her diet had clearly gone to pot.

'There's a school trip coming up.'

'I know. I can read.'

'Can I go on it?'

'No.'

'Other kids are going.'

'Other kids' mams might have more money than me.'

'It'll be a laugh.'

'I'm not paying good money just so you can have a laugh. You can watch the Comedy Channel instead.'

I'd chosen a bad time. Me mam was still hacked off with me for throwing Lanky Dave down the stairs, and for always having a go at her about FB.

'Please, Mam?'

She put a whole biscuit in her mouth. End of argument.

But if she wouldn't do it, maybe there was someone else who would.

Later, when me mam was in the bath.

'Callum?'

He looked surprised and put his can down. Don't normally talk to him.

'What is it, Danny?'

'There's a school trip coming up.'

'That's good.'

'But me mam says I cannit go on it.'

'Why not?'

'Too much money.'

'How much is too much?'

'Hundred and eighty quid.'

A smile split his fat face.

'I think we can stretch to that, General. I'll speak to your mum.'

Wazzocks.

After me mam got out of the bath FB spoke to her and next minute she stomped into me room with that face on that stops her looking pretty.

'Danny, what are you playing at?'

'What?' Like 'What, me, ref?' when you hack a player down and hope he didn't see.

'You know exactly what,' she said, her nose screwing up. 'Asking Callum to go on this trip.'

'He's got plenty of money.'

'Not the point.'

'He's going to be me step-dad, isn't he?'

Mam stared at me like she was trying to think of a better answer, but couldn't.

I'd got her.

'Can I go then?'

It took a while, but Mam finally said the one thing I wanted to hear.

'Okay, Danny, you can go.'

Eighteen

• •

Me plan had worked, but I was still worried sick.

I was going to be leaving me mam alone in the house with FB for a whole week. He hadn't hit her lately, in fact, not since before they'd decided to get married, but that didn't mean he wouldn't. With me not there who knew what he might do.

I did a couple of things to stop him. I hid his cans in the garage behind the lawnmower, and I emptied some of his vodka down the sink and filled the bottle up with water. Not sure that would do the trick. But it might.

'Excited about your trip, Danny?' said me mam, as she packed clean pants in me bag.

'Aye.'

Lying again. I was that nervous I'd barely swallowed half a dozen cornflakes. I'd also lied to Callum. I'd told him I needed cash for the school trip. Me jacket pocket was now bulging with money.

'Better go get the bus,' I said, trying to sound relaxed.

'No you won't, General,' said Callum. 'I'll run you down.'

'And I'm coming too.'

'But, Mam...'

'Don't you "But, Mam" me. We want to see you off, isn't that right, Callum?'

I needed another plan, quick. Went upstairs and sat on me bed to think, but me thinking didn't turn into anything useable. Me dad lived in Scotland. I was going to be heading in completely the wrong direction.

I grabbed me sports bag, climbed in the back of FB's Range Rover, fastened me seat belt, and we were off. Kept quizzing me brain. Give me an answer, give me an answer. But just like in school, nothing there. Me brain was officially broken.

FB drove into the school car park, fast, the way he does. We all got out. I was the slowest. Still thinking. Then an idea leaped into me head. Hoped it would work.

'Mam, I don't want you to see me off.'

'Why not?' she said, surprised.

Before I could tell her me lie, FB came to the rescue again.

'He's a teenager now, Kim. He doesn't want his mummy waving goodbye.'

I knew me mam wouldn't dare disagree with him.

'Suppose you're right. If that's what you want, Danny.'

Smiled. It's definitely what I want.

'Giz a hug, then,' she said.

I put me bag down and gave her a gigantic bear hug. I didn't want to let go. I was scared, for her, for me.

'I hope you're okay, Mam,' I whispered in her ear.

'I'll be fine, Danny.'

Looked over to make sure Callum wasn't listening. He was busy with a chamois leather on his wing mirror.

'If he tries anything, run out of the house. Don't let him hurt you.'

'Everything's gonna be okay.'

'Call Aunty Tina if he starts going mental.'

'I'm okay, Danny.'

Me mam was a bigger liar than me.

'I'll give you a call every night,' I said.

'That would be great.'

I finally let her go.

'I'll miss you, Danny.'

'I'll miss you too, Mam.'

'Love you.'

'Love you too.'

FB put his chamois down, walked over, and ruffled me hair with his fat hands, the way he does.

'Have a good trip, General,' he said. 'And try not to fall in any lakes.'

'Thanks, Callum.'

We stood still, looking at each other for ages, like we'd become photographs. Then I looked at the car. They got the hint. Me mam and FB each gave a little wave and walked off. Then she spotted Barry's mam. Looked like she wanted to talk to her, but Callum took her arm and walked her back to the car. They climbed in.

I needed them to disappear.

Saw me mam sitting there, looking sad. FB finally started the engine and drove off dead quick, just missing Mrs Darby, the music teacher.

Gone.

I waited till they'd turned into a speck before going towards the coaches parked in front of school. Mr Hetherington was checking names off a clipboard. Was so nervous I could hardy breathe. Mam had told the school I was up for the trip. I had to tell them different.

Joined the queue.

'What's that on your back?' said Mr Hetherington to Neil Thomas, a kid with a rucksack nearly as big as him. 'We're going to Cumbria, not climbing Mount Everest. Put your luggage in the coach and get on.'

Mr Hetherington crossed Neil's name off his list.

'That's a more sensible amount of luggage, Croft,' he said, looking at me bag.

'Thanks, sir, but I can't go, sir.'

Mr Hetherington hardly ever looks baffled, but he did now. 'Can't go? Why ever not?'

'Me gran's ill. I need to go and see her,' I said, super quick. You need to get lies out fast, so no one can spot them.

'Why have you brought that, then?' he said, looking at me bag.

'So I can stay over at her place.'

Could tell Mr Hetherington wanted to ask more questions. That's what teachers love doing. But a big queue had built up behind me. The coach was already late.

'Well, I'm really sorry to hear that, Danny.' I tried to look sad, instead of scared, which is what I really was. 'Maybe you can come on next year's trip,' he said. 'We're going to Scotland.'

Typical.

I picked up me bag and hurried away.

'Danny, where are you going?'

I turned. It was Amy.

'I cannit go on the trip.'

'Why not?' she said, her face crumpling.

Told her about me gran, the one with the imaginary illness.

'Oh, Danny, our first chance to go away together.'

'I'm sorry.'

I'd upset me mam. I'd upset Amy. Was that all I was good for? Upsetting people?

'Call me,' I said.

'I can't. They've said no phones on the trip. We can only borrow one in case of an emergency.'

A week away from Amy, and I couldn't even hear her voice. It was going to be torture. Had a quick look round to see that no one was watching and gave her hand a squeeze.

'Love you,' she mouthed.

'Love you too,' I mouthed back.

She hurried on to the coach. I turned and hurried across the car park.

'The coaches are that way, ya dafty.'

It was Lanky Dave, a plaster over his scar.

'I'm not going on the trip,' I said.

'Shame. I was looking forward to pushing you off a cliff.' Then a wicked smile crossed his face. 'On second thoughts, that is *fan*-tastic news. Me and Amy Reynolds together for a whole week. Lush.'

Lanky Dave headed for the coach, whistling.

I clenched me fists.

Nineteen

•

'Edinburgh, please.'

'Single?'

'Aye, just me.'

The gadgie behind the glass glared at me.

'Single is one way. Return means you're coming back.'

'Aye, I'm coming back.'

'When?'

'Next Saturday.'

'How old are you, son?'

'Seventeen.'

He looked at his computer and then at me again.

'Someone meeting you in Scotland?'

'Aye, me dad.'

He seemed happy enough with me answer. I gave him some money and he gave me the tickets.

He looked at his screen. 'There's a train in fifteen minutes.'

Even though I'd escaped the school trip, me heart hadn't stopped punching me chest all morning, like it had had enough of this stupid game and wanted out. It got even faster when I spotted a couple of coppers near the barriers. Don't know why. I hadn't done anything. Yet.

Found Platform Two. It was choc-a-bloc with people going away on holiday or for their jobs. I bet none of them were going to Edinburgh to do what I was going to do. I felt petrified just thinking about it, but it was too late to go back now.

The Edinburgh train pulled in. Got on and looked for an empty seat but couldn't find one anywhere. How crap is that? Pay all that money for a ticket and you don't even get a seat. That doesn't happen at the pictures, or McDonald's. Found a space on the floor near the toilets and sat on me bag. Two goths sat near me, students by the look. He had a goatee and she had dead long black hair and some metal in her nose. They were holding hands, kissing, touching. The girl's skin was smooth and white, like the tiles at the swimming baths. It didn't look like he'd ever bashed her.

Even though I hadn't eaten me breakfast I still felt sick. I was going a hundred and four miles to find a bloke I'd never met before to ask him to kill someone he'd never met before. Enough to make anyone want to puke. Me thoughts drifted off to Amy. I hoped she'd got a seat far away from Lanky Dave. Then I thought about me mam. FB had stopped her talking to Barry's mam. Would that put him in a mood? Was it enough to make him hit her?

Me bad thoughts were interrupted by a woman in a uniform shouting, 'Passengers from Newcastle.' I felt nervous again, like she knew what I was up to and would turn the train around. Not sure trains can do that, but they'd probably give it a good go. She looked down at me with a nothing face on, the way teachers do when they hand back your homework. I gave her me ticket. She clicked it with her clicker and gave it back. She didn't say a word, just went on. I let out me breath. The trip was proving a lot scarier than I thought.

Stood up and saw green fields flying past. Then I caught sight of the sea. I felt happy to spot that. Don't know why. Just did. I like the sea, me.

But the closer we got to Edinburgh the tighter me guts got. Bad thoughts crawled like worms inside me head. What if me dad's not there? What if he just slams the door in me face? What if he calls the police and tells them to take me back? I'd never thought any of these things before. Wish I'd never thought of them now.

Before I could worry meself stupid a woman's voice said, 'We are now approaching Edinburgh Waverley. Next stop: Edinburgh Waverley station.'

Here we go.

Edinburgh moved past quick, then slowed right down, then stopped, as if to say, *I'm ready for you now, bonny lad*. I picked up me bag and followed the kissing couple off the train and on to the platform. People were hurrying all over the place, like they knew where they were hurrying to. I didn't have a clue. There were loads of steps and bridges and escalators. No idea where they went, so I just kept following the crowds.

Went up an escalator and found meself outside on a street full of shops. I wondered if this was really Scotland. Hadn't seen one bloke in a skirt yet. But then I spotted one, outside a hotel. He had a skirt and a tartan blazer on. He looked dead Scotch.

Edinburgh didn't look really different, like Africa or somewhere, but it was different enough to make me feel scared. I didn't know the first thing about the place or how far away me dad lived. Checked on me phone. His house was way too far to walk. There were loads of buses going past but they all had weird names on the front. Decided to get a taxi. Only been in one a couple of times. No idea how much they cost. But thanks to Callum I was minted.

Climbed in.

'Where to, laddie?'

The driver spoke dead Scotch. I got the paper from me pocket. 'Steve Rivers. 9 Redwood Gardens, Newington, Edinburgh, marra.'

The driver grinned and drove off. I fastened me seat belt in case he drove nutty like FB.

'So you're a Geordie?' he said.

'Aye.'

'What brings you to Scotland?'

'Come to see me dad.'

'Does he work up here?'

'Think so.'

The Scotchman seemed confused by me answer and stopped asking questions. I looked out of the taxi window and saw a big castle on a hill. Funny how Newcastle doesn't have a castle and a town that isn't called Castle does. Edinburgh seemed to have hills all around it. I hoped it had a lake. Then I could take a picture of it, pretend it was the Lake District, and send it to me mam.

After driving for a bit, we turned off a big road down a smaller one full of massive stone houses. Then I saw a sign: *Redwood Gardens*. This was it.

I got the envelope from me jacket and paid the bloke. He said something so Scotch I couldn't make out a word. Gave him a bit more money in case he was swearing at me.

Grabbed me bag, climbed out the taxi and spotted number nine, a gigantic stone house across the street. Grinned. Me dad must have a great job to afford this. I walked up a long path to the red front door and saw a metal panel, with lots of names on it. What a wazzock. 'Course me dad didn't own the house, he lived in a flat. Aunty Tina had forgot to put that on the paper.

I spotted the name on the plate – *S Rivers*. I'd found him. Took a deep breath, like I was jumping off the pier at Whitley Bay, and pressed the button.

Nowt.

Pressed again.

Nowt.

Waited twenty seconds. Third time lucky?

Na.

It was Sunday. Me dad wouldn't work today, would he? S'pose he might. I let loose a groan. What if he works on a ship, or the oil rigs, or in the army? He might not be home for months. I only had six days. I thought of pressing the other buttons and asking the neighbours where he'd gone, but they'd probably tell me to get lost or worse, call the coppers. I was just going to have to wait.

I went to the other side of the road and sat on a wall so I could watch who came to the front door, like detectives do on telly. It was dead boring. I tried to see how long I could go without looking at me watch.

The longest was eighteen minutes, the shortest was twenty seconds. Don't think I'll ever be a detective.

A fat woman with three big plastic bags went in at 1.48 p.m. A girl with a tattoo on her neck went in at 2.16 p.m. Two kids in Man U tops went in at 3.15 p.m. Man U in Scotland? They're everywhere. Then an old bloke with a bent back and bandy legs went in at 3.27 p.m. Couldn't be me dad, could it? Never imagine me mam having a bairn with that.

By now I was clammin. Why didn't I get me mam to make me some bait? I didn't want to go look for a shop in case I missed him, so I just sat and watched house nine. Just waiting, waiting, waiting. I remember once going to bingo with me mam. I was waiting for one number – fourteen. It never came. Waiting for nine was like that.

Before long it got dark.

I was starting to hate this place.

6.36 p.m. to 7.45 p.m. Four more people came to the door, two newspaper boys on bikes, a little woman with a limp, and a gadgie with a walking stick. But no one who looked like he might be me dad.

7.49 p.m. Spotted a bloke walking down the street carrying a plastic bag. Couldn't tell what he was like in the dark, just that he was a bloke. I crossed me fingers.

'Go into nine, go into nine,' I whispered.

Crossed fingers did it.

The bloke turned up the path towards the door. I jumped off the wall, grabbed me bag and ran over the road. Got closer. It was still too dark to make him out. The bloke took a key from his pocket and went for the lock.

This time, please.

'Steve?'

He turned. There was just enough light to see him. He had a young face.

'Aye.'

'Steve Rivers?'

'Aye.' He looked confused. 'Who are you?'

Swallowed what little spit I could find.

'Me name's Danny. I'm your son.'

Twenty

• •

'What the hell are you doing here?' he shouted, in Scotch.

Not the welcome I was expecting.

'I've come to see you.'

'Why?'

'I just have.'

'Heaven help me.'

Me dad wasn't the only one in shock. I was too. He was nothing like I'd expected him to be. I thought me dad would be big – everywhere. Big head, big arms, big body, the lot, like the dads you see at school. But he was short and skinny, not even a beer belly. I also thought he'd be older, bald maybe, with a beard, but he had a baby face. He didn't look much older than me.

He stared at me for a long time, probably hoping I'd disappear, but I didn't, I just stood there, looking back at him. He seemed really panicked, scanning the street with quick looks.

'You'd better come in,' he said.

I followed him into the stone house. The hall was cold, like being outside, a couple of rusty old bikes up against a wall, paint falling off the walls, and the floor carpeted in junk mail. He turned on a light and we went up stair after stair after stair till we came to a landing. Saw a sign. *Flat C. Rivers.* This was where he lived.

He got his key out and opened his front door. The builders had forgotten to put a hall in. We went straight from outside into the front room. The flat was even smaller than the place me mam and me used to live in. Looked about. But there wasn't much to see. One titchy sofa, a chair, a telly, a table. That was it. So much for me dad being minted.

'Sit,' said Steve, as if I was a dog.

He looked mad, like FB does when he gets spit on his lips. Hoped he wouldn't hit me.

'Did she send you?' he went, putting his plastic bag on the floor. I guessed 'she' was me mam.

'Na.'

Steve looked even more confused.

'You came here on your own?'

Nodded. I thought he might be proud of that, but he wasn't.

'For crying out loud,' he went. 'She hasn't moved up here, has she?'

'Na, still lives in Gateshead.'

'Does she know where you've gone?'

'Na.'

He gave his watch a worried look.

'It's nearly eight o'clock. She'll be wondering where the hell you are. She'll call the pollis.'

'No, she won't. She thinks I'm on the school trip.'

'What school trip?'

'The one I'm meant to be on in the Lake District.'

'Won't your teachers know you're missing?'

'No, they think I've gone to me gran's.'

'This is doing my wee head in.' Steve flopped down next to me. 'Who told you I was here?' he said, angry. 'Who told you?'

Didn't want to tell him, but thought I'd better.

'Aunty Tina.'

'Who the hell's that?'

'Me mam's sister.'

Me dad rubbed his little chin, as he took it all in. 'Tina Croft. She was a mate of my sister. Didn't even know those two were still in touch.' He bit a fingernail. 'Seems like you can't trust anyone any more.'

Always thought me mam must have told Aunty Tina where me dad lived. Maybe she had no idea where he'd gone.

Me dad turned back to me.

'So what in God's name have you come here for?'

Didn't want to tell him. Too early for that.

'Just wanted to see me dad.'

'Well, you've seen him. Now you can clear off back to Gateshead.'

This was not how I'd expected things to go. Thought I'd get to Edinburgh and find me dad, me big dad. He'd give me a massive hug, tell me all the things he'd done, then he'd make me tea, we'd watch some telly, then I'd tell him what I wanted from him. He'd say, 'Why aye, son,' and that would be that. I hadn't expected this, not in me worst dreams. I didn't want to look at him, me small, skinny, angry dad, so I stared at the floor instead.

Crying is so embarrassing. It's like being sick before you can make it to the bog. But sometimes, even though you try with all your might, you just can't stop it. I'd tricked me mam, I'd tricked FB, I'd tricked the school, I'd tricked Amy, I'd come all the way to Scotland to find me dad, and guess what? He didn't want to see me. On top of that I was scared and tired and hungry. If that's not worth crying for, nothing is.

'Oh, for the love of Jesus,' he said.

I looked up and saw three of him through the tears.

'I just wanted to see you, that's all.'

'Listen,' he went, squinting at his watch again, 'it's too late for you to be going back tonight. You can sleep on the sofa, but you're going back tomorrow, do you hear me?'

'The school trip's on for a week.'

'I don't give a monkey's bum about your school trip, you're going back tomorrow.' He had a big voice for a skinny bloke. 'God, what am I gonna tell Megan?'

'Who's Megan?'

'My fiancée, the fiancée who has absolutely no idea I've got a kid.'

I thought I'd thought this through, but I hadn't, I'd cocked it right up. I never stopped to think he might have a lass, a lass who'd never even heard of me.

'Why didn't you tell her?' I said, wiping me nose on me sleeve.

'Because I came to Edinburgh to start a new life. The reason I settled here was to get away from the past.'

I guess that meant me.

'Why?'

'What's it to you? I just did, okay? I didn't ask for this. Tomorrow you're going back to Tyneside.'

'Can't I stay a bit longer? Please?'

'No,' he screamed.

Things had just gone from bad to worse. Tomorrow I was going to be sent home. How would I talk me way out of that one? Before I had time to think the front door opened and a lass walked in. She looked about the same age as me mam. She had short legs, short blonde hair, and two heavy shopping bags. She also had a funny look on her face.

'Stevie, what's going on?' she said.

She sounded even more Scotch than me dad.

'Megan, er, this, this is my cousin, Danny. He's paying us a quick visit.'

Megan didn't seem very happy to see me.

'How quick?'

'Six days,' I said, butting in.

I knew I shouldn't have said that, but it was the only thing I could think of to keep me plan working.

'Six days?' she said, her face screwed up.

From the corner of me eye I could see Steve clench his fists, looking dead angry, like he wanted to bash me.

'I heard shouting from the hall,' she said.

'Just joking, weren't we, Danny?'

'Aye, just joking,' I said, putting me best false smile on.

'Where's he going to sleep?'

'Sofa,' I said.

If this was a shocked face competition it was a dead heat between these two.

Megan stopped staring at me and turned her stare on Steve. 'How come you didn't tell me he was coming?'

'Forgot.'

'Forgot?' said Megan, looking at me. 'But he's only a kid.'

'I'm fourteen.'

'That's what I said.'

'It slipped my mind,' said Steve.

'It slipped your mind that your cousin was coming to stay with us all week?'

Steve shifted on his feet, like he was walking barefoot on pebbles. 'It's a wee surprise.'

'Surprises like this I can do without.' And with that she stormed off into the kitchen with her bags.

Steve was fuming. He came right up close to me, so close I could feel the hot from his mouth, and whispered, loud in me ear.

'You little bastard.'

Then he went into the kitchen, and slammed the door.

Twenty-One

• • •

Steve and Megan had a massive argument. Was just like being at home, except this time the big voice belonged to Megan, and the small voice belonged to Steve. I tried to listen at the door, but the wood got in the way. Even if it hadn't I'm not sure I'd have worked it out, because they'd gone even more Scotch. I needed an English–Scotch dictionary.

Made out a few bits.

'Can't afford…' Big voice.

'Few days…' Little voice.

'Not a hotel…' Big voice.

'Just a kid…' Little voice.

'Didn't tell me…' Big voice.

I thought of grabbing me bag and heading back to Tyneside, but what would I say to me mam? The Lake District was too cold so they sent us all home? She'd find out that the trip was still on and I'd be in an even bigger world of cack than the one I was in now.

After a bit the voices in the kitchen got quieter, and a bit after that the door opened and Megan came out with a tray of food.

'Do you like pizza, Danny?'

Was that hungry I'd eat owt.

'Aye.'

Megan put the tray down on me knee. 'Thanks.'

She turned the telly on and sat next to me on the sofa. Steve stayed in the kitchen. I thought I heard a beer can *fsssh*. I felt a bit sorry for him, getting shouted at for something he didn't do. Just like me mam when FB goes off on one. But then he should have told Megan the truth. He should have told her about me. Not like I never happened.

I finished me tea, and Megan picked up me tray.

'Thanks,' I said again.

'You're welcome.'

She went back into the kitchen to carry on the argument.

I looked at me watch. 9.14 p.m. OMG. I hadn't phoned me mam. She might have called the teachers. They'd say, 'But Danny's not here, Miss Croft.' They'd work out that all that stuff about me gran being ill was a bag of lies.

I grabbed me phone from me sports bag, opened the door and sat on the stairs. I pressed the buttons dead fast, like FB.

Me mam answered after one ring.

'Hello,' she said, sounding scared.

'Hi, Mam.'

'What happened, Danny? I've been worried sick.'

'Been busy, unpacking.'

Her voice then went a bit more normal.

'So how was the coach trip?'

'Okay.'

'What's the weather like?'

'Wet.' A guess. It's called the Lake District, so can't be far wrong.

'So what's your room like?'

'Square.'

Mam gave a little laugh. 'Are you sharing?'

'Aye.'

'I hope the girls are in a separate room.'

'Aye.'

I should get a medal for lying, me.

'Had your tea?'

'Aye.'

'Do you know any words other than "aye"?'

'Aye.'

Me mam sighed. Needed to change the subject.

'Where's Callum?'

'What are you doing tomorrow?'

Callum was there, listening.

'I want you to be safe, Mam.'

'Wear your boots if you're going climbing.'

'Did you hear what I said, Mam?'

'And don't do anything silly.'

'If he does anything, lock yourself in the bathroom. Or the bedroom.'

'And take care on those rocks. They could be slippy.'

'Promise me. If he tries anything, run out of the house. Or call Aunty Tina.'

'And wear something warm.'

'Go into another room, Mam. I want to know you're going to be safe.'

'I'd better be off, Danny. Sleep well. Love you.'

'Love you too, Mam.'

'Where have my bloody beer cans gone?' Callum.

'I'm going to have to go,' said me mam, her voice sounding shaky.

Click. Gone.

The words I'd overheard made me feel sick. What did I have to go and hide his stupid beer for? He'll think me mam's done it. He'll bash her for sure. He loves his beer.

I thought of ringing her back and owning up. But

he'd still hit her for having such a bastard kid. Every single thing I ever do is wrong.

Went back into the flat. Steve and Megan were still in the kitchen, rowing. Is that all grown-ups ever do? Lay on the sofa, thinking about what might be happening back in Gateshead. FB had sometimes gone mental over nothing, like water down his shorts and being asked not to drive home mortal drunk. What would he do to me mam if he found his beer had gone missing?

Two women killed every week.

I turned the telly on and found some football. It was Scotch football, but I still watched it. The voices in the kitchen got quieter, like they'd got tired of being loud, and the door opened. Steve came and sat next to me. He whispered in me ear again. This time the whisper smelled of beer.

'You have dropped me right in it.'

Couldn't argue with that.

We just sat and watched the match. After half-time Megan came in carrying a tray with a small bowl of pasta on it. She was probably on a diet, like me mam. She joined us on the sofa. All three squashed together. Nobody said anything for a long time.

Megan finally did.

'Is it your first time in Scotland, Danny?'

'Aye.'

And hopefully the last.

Megan wiped some sauce off her top. 'What are you two going to do all week?'

'No idea,' said me dad.

'If the weather was a bit warmer you could have gone across to Loch Lomond. Bet Danny would like that.'

Bet Danny wouldn't.

The silence came back.

And that's how I spent me first ever night in Scotland, on a sofa next to two grumpy Scotch people I'd never met before, watching Motherwell v Partick Thistle.

Twenty-Two

•

Didn't sleep much that night. Strange bed, strange place, strange situation.

On top of that I couldn't stop worrying about me mam.

Thought Steve and Megan might have got tired of arguing, but when I woke up they were still at it. Must be going for the world record longest argument. Except in this house it was the woman doing all the shouting.

I checked me phone hoping maybe Amy had got hers back from the teachers. Me luck was out. Nothing. I got dressed. Did it quick in case Megan came in. Then I sat on the sofa wondering what to do next. After a bit

Megan came out. She was different, had a long skirt on, Puffa jacket, little black shoes, make-up.

'Have you had your breakfast, Danny?'

Shook me head.

'Well, help yourself. The cereal's in the cupboard next to the cooker.'

She seemed nice. Not like Steve.

Megan picked up a bag from a peg on the wall and went to the door. 'See yous later.'

'Aye.'

Slam.

I went in the kitchen and found the cupboard and the cornflakes. Then I took me bowl through to the sofa. Just got me first mouthful in when the bedroom door opened. Steve walked in. He had a T-shirt and boxers on. Looked even skinnier than last night, more like a lad than a dad. I couldn't even spot a tattoo. You've got to be hard to have tattoos. Barry's dad's covered in them.

I thought he might be in a better mood than last night. Wrong again.

'You have an evil streak a mile long,' he said.

Didn't like strangers talking at me like that, but I suppose Steve was different, he was me dad.

'Sorry, Steve.'

'The name's Stevie.'

Don't know why he'd added an extra letter. Seemed like a waste of time. But he'd done it anyway.

Stevie ignored the chairs and sat on the floor, wiping his face with his hands again and again. Then he glared at me.

'What in God's name am I gonna do with you?'

I tried to eat me cornflakes, but couldn't, not with him sitting there with that look.

'Why're you so angry with me?'

Stevie laughed.

'Put yourself in my shoes, Danny,' he said. 'Put yourself in my wee shoes. Imagine for one moment, someone you've never met before, turns up, unexpected, uninvited, and wants to stay for a week.'

'I'm not just someone.'

Think he knew I'd come up with a good answer.

Then I came up with a good question.

'Why did you leave me mam?'

Stevie bit his nails, what was left of them, and sat there, staring at nothing.

'I said…'

'I heard what you said,' snapped Stevie. 'Wasn't a case of wanting to leave your mam, was a case of having to.'

'Eh?'

He took a big swig of air. 'Your mam was only fifteen. I was just sixteen.' No wonder he looks so young. 'We were kids, and to put the icing on the cake, we weren't even going out. We got drunk at a party. She got pregnant. Imagine how that went down.'

'Like the Titanic.'

'Exactly.'

'So because you and me mam had it off you had to leave?'

'We didn't just have it off, Danny. We had you, we had a bairn.'

'And you went to live in Scotland.'

'Not went to live, sent to live.'

'Just because of me?'

'More to it than that, Danny, a helluva lot more. Have you heard of the black sheep of the family?'

Nodded.

'Well, that was me, the blackest sheep in the field, probably the whole bloody county. Me mam used to say we should get a key cut for the coppers. They were round that often.'

'What did you do?'

Could tell he didn't want to spit it out. But he did.

'Stealing cars. Setting fire to stuff. Shoplifting.'

Stared at him, a grin on me face. Couldn't believe me skinny little dad had done all that.

'It's nothing to be proud of, Danny.'

'Did the coppers not get you?'

'Only ever got caught for the smaller stuff. More by luck than good judgement. I was that close to going inside,' he said, his two fingers nearly touching. 'Your mam getting pregnant was the last straw. My parents had had a bellyful of me, so they sent me to live with my Uncle Connor and Aunty Fiona up here in Edinburgh.' His face told me the memory was messing with his head. 'They knocked me into shape, eventually.'

'Do your mam and dad not come and see you?'

Stevie shook his head.

'They're not together any more. Mam rings me once a year on my birthday. My sister's been up a couple of times. Dad wants nothing to do with me.'

'Did me mam not want you to stay?'

'No, she did not want me to stay, Danny. She wanted nothing to do with me.'

'But she must have liked you to…'

Stevie laughed again.

'Booze does funny things to people.'

Knew that much. Except what happens afterwards isn't funny.

Wondered if FB had found the cans yet. Wondered if me mam was covered in bruises. Wondered why I'd done such a stupid thing.

'Kim never really liked me. She liked me even less when she found I'd got her up the duff.'

'But didn't you want to see me?'

Stevie bit what little was left of his fingernail.

'Not an option, Danny. I couldn't go back to Tyneside.'

'Not even for me birthday?'

'Not even for your birthday.'

Things were finally starting to make sense.

'You must have been dead angry when they sent you to Scotland.'

'At first, I had a lot of mates in Gateshead, but they were the wrong type of mates. If I'd stayed there I'd have been up to my ears in it. I started again up here. For the last fourteen years I've been trying to forget about everything that went on down there.'

He stared at me.

'But it seems like my past has finally caught up with me.'

Twenty-Three

• •

Stevie rang his work and, with a straight face, told them he had a bad virus. Can you have a good virus? He made his voice go a bit funny, and told them he wouldn't be in for a few days. Maybe I got me lying from him.

He put the phone down and leaned against the wall.

'What's your job?' I said.

Hoped he might say bouncer, or fireman, or soldier.

'I work in a sandwich shop.' Stevie spotted me face wasn't happy. 'Not what you thought your dad would do, eh?'

'Hadn't really thought about it.' Lie number six million for that week.

'I hope you bloody appreciate what I'm doing for you.'

He hadn't done anything yet. But I decided not to make him go radgy again.

'Thanks,' I said.

Stevie walked over and grabbed his leather jacket off the peg.

'I'm not going to sit here all day with a wee Geordie staring at me. Let's go to the zoo.'

I'd rather play football, but it was better than stopping in. I grabbed me coat and we went down all the stairs to the street. Thought we might be getting the bus to the zoo, but Stevie walked a few steps, stopped by a blue Mini parked on the road, and unlocked the doors.

'Don't just look at it,' he said.

We got in, Stevie started it and we headed off. He drove much slower than FB. Suppose you don't need to drive fast if your job's cutting bread, unless someone needs an emergency sandwich.

Thought of another question for Stevie.

'Do you like Formula One?'

'Hate it.'

Result.

I wanted to know more about the 'other' Stevie, the one who had the coppers round all the time, the one who got booted out of Gateshead, the one who was too bad to marry me mam. If he was that bad, he'd have no problem sorting out FB.

'So did you batter anybody?'

'Will you shut your wee gob about that? I've moved on, do you hear? I'm not talking about it.'

Me told.

Stevie didn't say much as he drove. I thought I'd try and be friendly.

'Do you like living in Scotland?'

'It's okay. Like everywhere, good points, bad points.'

'You've got a Scotch accent.'

'It's not Scotch, that's whisky. It's Scots.'

Never knew that.

'So how come you don't talk Geordie no more?'

'Lived here a long time, Danny. I guess it's all part of the new Stevie, the new improved Stevie.'

'So how long have you and Megan been going out?'

'Three years.' He smiled when he said this, like his head was thinking of her. 'She's a top lass. Means the world to me.'

'I've got a lass.'

'Have you?' said Stevie, surprised.

'Aye, Amy Reynolds. She's dead bonny.'

'Well, don't make the same mistake I made.'

After driving for a bit Stevie turned into Edinburgh Zoo, and we joined a queue at the ticket office. Stevie paid. I said thanks. Mam always tells me to say that, though I nearly always forget.

Stevie opened up a little map of the zoo. 'Where do you want to go first?'

Only one answer.

'Lions.'

'Lions it is.'

The lions were right at the top of the zoo. We walked up loads of twisty paths till we found their den. They were Asiatic ones. You can also have African lions but the zoo didn't have any of them. Maybe they couldn't afford them. Probably spent all their money on penguins and stuff.

In the wild lions run dead fast, jump on deer and eat them. They act a bit different in Scotland, just wandering round, looking a bit bored. But I knew that they could still tear your head off in a flash. Shame me mam didn't have one. I kept thinking about what I'd heard on the phone last night, wondering what he'd done to her.

We watched the lions for about twenty minutes. Should have saved them till last. Monkeys, zebras, koalas, birds, are nothing compared to lions. We went down the hill and saw a couple of big pools with lots of penguins waddling around and swimming. A girl in a uniform threw fish to them. They caught them like world-class keepers, in their gobs, and swallowed the whole lot without even chewing. Penguins must get real gut rot.

'Has your mam got a boyfriend?'

'Aye.'

'What's he do?'

Hits her.

'He's into computers.'

Stevie nodded like this was a good job. Suppose it's better than sandwiches.

'Does she ever talk… about me?'

'Never.'

I looked at Stevie to see if he was angry about this, but he wasn't. Just staring at the penguins. Time to ask Stevie an important question.

'Do you think you'll ever go back to Gateshead?'

'There's nothing there for me.'

'There's me.'

Not sure I should have said that, but it was too late. Words are like helium balloons, once you let them go you can't get them back.

Stevie didn't say anything for a bit, like he was thinking about what I'd said.

'Do you want to go see the pandas?' he said.

'Why?'

'Because they're as rare as square eggs, that's why.'

Could tell Stevie was keen on the idea, so off we went to the panda den. One of them, the boy panda, was asleep under a pile of leaves, but the girl panda was awake, lying on a ledge.

'They're amazing, aren't they?' said Stevie.

Couldn't see what was amazing about them. They were just lying there, not like they were juggling balls or riding bicycles or anything.

'So where are the other pandas?' I said, looking round.

'There are only two of them, Sweetie and Sunshine. They're hoping they'll breed.'

'If they want them to breed, why are they in different cages?'

'They only breed for two days a year.'

'Pandas are weird. I like their colours, though.'

Stevie found a café. I had sausage, chips, beans, a biscuit and a cola. Stevie just had a coffee. No wonder he's so skinny. He didn't say much while I was eating. I needed to get him on my side. Decided to talk about football.

'So which team do you support?'

'Hibs.'

'What sort of name's that?'

'A great name. They were founded by an Irishman. Hibernian is the Roman name for Ireland.'

'A Scottish football team called Ireland, that's mental.'

'Suppose you support the Toon?'

Grinned and nodded. It made me feel good, just thinking about them.

After the zoo we went back to Stevie's flat. I needed to find out how strong he was.

'How many press-ups can you do?'

'Press-ups, how the hell should I know? Twenty, maybe a few more.'

'Let's see you, then.'

'You cheeky bampot.'

'So you can't do any, then?'

''Course I can.'

Stevie rolled up his sleeves, pulled the sofa out of the way, got down on the floor, and off he went. I did the counting.

'One, two, three, four, five, six, seven, eight, nine…'

Stevie stopped and held himself up on straight arms, panting like a dog in a hot car.

'Told you you couldn't do it.'

'I'll show you,' he grunted.

Off he went again.

'Ten, eleven, twelve, thirteen, fourteen, fifteen…'

Just when I thought he was going to do it Stevie's arms collapsed and he fell on his face on the carpet. Not sure he'd ever beat FB in a fight. But for the first time since I got here I saw Stevie laugh, a proper laugh, like you do when someone falls over on the telly.

The front door opened and Megan walked in, shaking a brolly. She looked down at Stevie on the floor.

'What in God's name's going on?'

'Press-ups,' he said.

'You're a numpty, Stevie Rivers.'

Megan went in the kitchen while me and Stevie sat

on the sofa watching telly. Smells told us food was on the way. Stevie went and got some trays and we all sat down with tea on our knees. Chicken in breadcrumbs with chips.

'So how was your day, fellas?' said Megan.

'Canny.'

'Where'd you go?'

'The zoo,' said Stevie.

'Poor animals,' said Megan. 'They shouldn't be locked up.'

Especially not in Scotland.

'It's keeping them alive,' said Stevie.

'Yes, but in a cage.'

'Life imprisonment is better than the death penalty.'

Megan shook her head as if she wasn't sure. Don't think she'll be going to see the pandas.

'So what yous doing tomorrow?' she asked.

'What do you fancy doing, Danny?' said Stevie.

'Dunno, Dad.'

Wazzocks. Times a million.

Twenty-Four

• • •

Didn't think three little letters could cause so much trouble, but they had.

Megan screamed the place down, then threw her dinner all over the floor. 'Stevie,' she shouted. 'Tell me what is going on, right now.'

I guess Stevie could have said, 'He's only joking', but he wasn't quick enough. It's easier to lie when you've got time to plan. But when you get caught, like at school, it's hard to lie right. That's what happened to Stevie. He just went as white as his plate, then looked at me like I was the worst thing in the world.

'I don't know what is going on,' he said slowly.

Megan glared at him, the veins in her neck sticking out like the wires round the back of the telly.

'He's not lying, is he?' she said. 'He's telling the truth, he's your son.'

It took a long time coming, but Stevie finally did a nod.

'I should have known all that stuff about him being your cousin was complete nonsense.'

Megan looked at the ceiling, the door, me, the telly, like she didn't know where to send her eyes. But she still had that mad look on her face, as if she was going to hit him, or me, or anyone else who turned up.

'Somebody wake me up from this nightmare,' she said. 'What have you brought him here for, Stevie, and why now? We're supposed to be getting married.'

Don't think Stevie liked that word 'supposed', as in they might not. He shook his head. Looked one hundred per cent miserable. 'It's a long story.'

'Good thing we've got all night, then, isn't it?' said Megan, nostrils flaring like a bull ready to charge. 'How long have we been going out?'

'Three years.'

'Yes, three years, and in that time we've talked about the weather, celebrities, politics, music, sport, loads of stuff. Funny how you couldn't find a few seconds to mention one rather important fact: that you're a father.'

I wondered if Stevie had told her he also used to be

dead bad. Better not say anything about that. She'd kill him.

'I had a one-night stand back in Gateshead when I was sixteen. The girl got pregnant. Everyone in the family was furious.'

'Can't imagine why. And how old was she?'

'Fifteen.'

'Oh, this just keeps getting better and better.'

'Mam and Dad had had enough of me, so I got sent to Edinburgh to live with Uncle Connor and Aunty Fiona. I never saw the girl again. Never saw the boy again, till now. End of story.'

'No, not end of story, Stevie, start of story. Unless you hadn't noticed, your little bit of history has just returned. Your flesh and blood is sleeping on our bloody sofa.'

'I didn't ask him to come.'

'Oh, and that makes it all right, does it? Because he's your uninvited child it's somehow all right?'

There were tears in Megan's eyes. She tried to screw them away, but they wouldn't go. She turned her red eyes on me.

'If Stevie didn't invite you, what did you come here for?'

Thought it best not to tell her.

'Just wanted to see me... dad.'

'No, you want money,' said Megan, staring at me, like I was some sort of monster. 'Child support, that's what

147

this is about, isn't it? Your ma sent you here. You're after money, it's always about money.' Megan looked around the flat and laughed. 'What bloody money?'

'She didn't send me here. I came by meself.'

'You expect me to believe that?'

'It's the truth.'

'But she knows you're here, right?'

Shook me head.

'Oh, Heaven save me, he's a runaway. The poliss'll be after him.'

'They won't. She thinks I'm on a school trip.'

Megan's mouth dropped open like a ventriloquist's dummy.

'He's telling the truth, Meg,' said Stevie.

'That's big, coming from you, a man who's been lying through his teeth all these years.' Megan looked back at me. 'So if she didn't send you, who told you where Stevie lived?'

'Me Aunty Tina. Nobody else would say. She thought I was just going to write to him.'

The room fell quiet, apart from the man on the telly, who was talking about making puddings. Stevie broke the silence.

'I'm sorry, Meg.'

'I thought I could trust you, Stevie. When exactly were you going to tell me all this? At the altar? Signing the register? On our honeymoon?'

Stevie heaved out a big breath. 'If you want the truth, Meg, I was never going to tell you. It happened such a long time ago. It was all a mistake, one great massive mistake.' Hated being called that. 'I thought I could just bury it. Haven't you ever done something in the past you don't want to talk about?'

'Aye, but nothing quite like this. Not a bairn, Stevie, not a bloody bairn. She sniffed. 'So what else have you failed to tell me?'

'Nothing, Meg,' he lied. 'That's it.'

Stevie went over and tried to put his hand on Megan's but she slapped it away.

'Let's talk about this in private,' said Stevie. 'Let's go to The Stag.'

Megan looked at the food on the floor. The sauce had sunk into the carpet, like blood. It would take ages to clean up, but I don't think she was that bothered. Then she turned to me.

'What about him?'

'He got to Scotland on his own. Reckon he can sit in a flat by himself for a few hours.'

Megan nodded.

Stevie went over to the pegs, took two coats down, then looked at me, an evil face on, like he wanted to kill me.

Slam.

Gone.

I normally like the telly on when I'm on me own, but not tonight. I switched the Scotsman off. It was dead quiet. All I could hear was the breath coming out me nose. I couldn't believe what had just happened. We'd had a good day, considering he didn't want me within a million miles of him. All I'd said was one word. And what's wrong with saying 'Dad'? I mean, he is.

Needed to call me mam.

Press. Press. Press.

Ring. Ring. Ring.

'Hello.'

'Hi, Mam,' I said, trying hard to sound normal.

'Oh, hi, Danny,' said me mam, in her nice call-centre voice. 'How's it going, pet?'

Could tell that FB wasn't around.

'Okay.'

Then her voice changed.

'Danny, did you hide Callum's beer in the garage?'

What could I say, the cans sprouted wings and flew there?

'Yes, Mam.'

'Callum was angry, really angry.'

Didn't even want to think what that could mean.

'Did he…?'

'No, Danny. I told him I needed more room in the fridge. Said the garage was cold enough this time of year.'

Proud of me mam. Just as sneaky as me.

'I just wish you'd told me what you'd done, Danny.'

'Sorry, Mam. I was just…'

'I know what you were doing.'

Silence.

She didn't want to talk about it. The subject that could never be turned into words.

'So what did you do today?' she asked.

'Went out.'

'Of course you went out, you're in the Lake District. Not the sort of place you stay in. What's the weather like?'

I grabbed the paper from the sofa, and found the weather for the Lake District. 'It was cool, eight degrees. Sunny spells with a few showers. Light westerly winds.'

'You sound like the weatherman.'

Lucky she didn't check. I'd read the wrong paper. That was yesterday's weather.

'Bet there's lots of snoring in your room.'

'Aye.'

'And other sounds.'

'Aye.'

'When you study English do you ever use any other words than "aye"?'

'Aye.'

Mam laughed. For about a second.

She knows. Mams always know.

'Just a bit homesick, I bet.'

'Aye.'

'You'll call me tomorrow night?'

'Aye.'

'Love you, Danny.'

'Love you too, Mam.'

But she hadn't finished yet.

'And in future before you do anything stupid, you promise you'll tell me first?'

Twenty-Five

•

I woke with a jump.

For a minute I couldn't figure out where on earth I was. Then I heard mumbly Scottish voices, and it all tumbled back into me head – the train, Edinburgh, the flat, Stevie, Megan, me, Dad. They were still arguing about that word.

I looked around. The telly was off, so were the lights, the food had gone from the floor, and there was a blanket on me, a thick tartan one. I got up, put me clothes on and sat on the sofa. Was thinking about Amy and Lanky Dave when the bedroom door opened. It was Megan. She had her dress and a jacket on.

She didn't look as pretty as yesterday, her hair all messy, her cheeks white, her eyes squidged tight. She had one of those little cases with a long handle for people who are too lazy to carry them.

'Morning, Danny.'

It wasn't a smiley voice. It was a voice that said, *This is all your fault.*

'Morning, Megan.'

She pulled her case towards the door.

'You going away?' I said.

'Aye.'

'Somewhere nice?'

'Cowdenbeath. Not that nice.'

For a horrible moment I thought her and Stevie might both be going to Cowdenbeath without me. I didn't fancy being stuck in Scotland on me own for a week, with just a Scottish telly.

'Is Stevie going?'

Megan shook her head.

'When you coming back?'

'I don't know, Danny, I just don't know.'

She opened the door, wheeled her case out and slammed the door behind her, *wham*, before I could find out.

Quiet.

I lay back on the sofa looking at the ceiling. Spotted a spider. Wondered if he talked Scottish. Be funny if he did. The bedroom door opened again. This time it was

Stevie. He had red boxers on. They matched his eyes. He came and sat on the floor next to the sofa, where the food had been. Hope they'd wiped it up properly. He sat staring at nothing, like he was a zombie.

'Megan's gone to Cowdenbeath,' I said, in case he didn't know.

He looked at me, like I was speaking foreign.

'She's gone to her ma's,' he said slowly.

'Not gone on her holidays?'

'No, Danny, Megan has not gone on her holidays. She's left me.'

Now that I had a girlfriend I knew how Stevie must be feeling. I also knew that it was mostly my fault. Megan would still be here if I'd kept me mouth shut. The rest of the fault belonged to Stevie. He should have told her.

'Why didn't you tell her?'

Stevie exploded.

'It's none of your business what I tell, or don't tell, my girlfriend, fiancée.'

Stevie's eyes had tears, but he killed them with his knuckles. His face was red like he'd been stung by bumblas. Didn't look like a boy any more, he looked more like a man, an angry man.

He got up and walked around the room. Then he sat down again. This time he couldn't stop the tears. Great big ones running down his blotchy face on to his bare belly.

'I don't want her to go, Danny. I want her back.'

She'd only been gone ten minutes.

Stevie found a box of tissues from under the *Daily Record* and blew his nose, a gigantic snotty blow, like Barry does after football.

'We were going to get married next summer. What did you have to say that for?'

'Just slipped out.'

'Wish it had stayed in.'

'She called me a liar, but it wasn't a lie, Danny,' he said, his voice going wobbly, 'I just kept her in the dark, that's all. I'd never lie to her.'

'Still think you shoulda told her.'

'You'll do things in your life, Danny, that you won't want to talk about. Mark my words, that'll happen, then you'll understand.'

Stevie just sat, looking at the turned-off telly, like there was something good on. I didn't know what to do. They never teach you stuff like this at school. Just things that are totally useless, like French or history. I went to the kitchen and had some cornflakes. Me plans had all been destroyed. Me dad had turned out to be as soft as clarts, I'd made his girlfriend leave by saying 'Dad', and now he'd gone mad, watching a switched-off telly.

I stayed in the kitchen for two hours and twenty-nine minutes. Know because I kept looking at me watch.

I was dead bored. Thought about going for a walk, but I didn't know where I was, and didn't even have a key to get back in. But I had to do something. Opened the kitchen door. He was still there, with a nothing look on his face. I saw a man do that at Grey's Monument, once, dressed as a statue, not moving, just staring. People put coins in his hat. A statue, imagine doing that? People have some stupid jobs.

'What are we doing today?' Stevie said nothing. 'What we doing today?'

'Were you sent here to destroy me?'

'What?'

'I said, were you sent here to destroy me, like in the movies?'

Was starting to feel scared.

Stevie stood up, his chest puffed out.

'Right, Danny, you are going back to Gateshead.'

'I can't, me mam'll kill me.'

'If she doesn't, I will. You're going back.'

'I'm not gannin.'

'You are. I'm taking you to the station.'

Stevie grabbed me arm. Then he put his face so close it went blurred.

'You have overstayed your welcome, you are leaving. Now.'

I sat down on the sofa, but he put his hands round me waist and lifted me up. He was dead strong for a skinny bloke, but I wasn't going to let him throw me out, not after all I'd done to get here. Started waving me arms about and kicking me legs like crazy. Me foot bashed him hard on the knee, and he dropped me on the sofa. Turned around. I'd never seen a face so angry. His fists were balled tight. Spit on his lips. He looked just like Callum.

Then he lifted his hand to hit me.

Twenty-Six

• •

Closed me eyes, expecting the blow any second. But it never came. Stevie was still there, in front of me, but his arms were by his sides, and his hands were no longer fists.

'I thought you were going to hit me.'

'So did I,' said Stevie. 'So did I.'

'I divvent want to go back to Gateshead.'

'So you keep saying.' He let out two big puffs of air from his nose. 'I'm gonna let you stay.'

I didn't think he'd ever change his mind, not in a million years. But sometimes the things in life you think won't ever happen actually happen. Could hardly believe me lugs.

'Honest?'

'Honest.'

This is what is officially known as a miracle.

'Listen, Danny. I have no idea why you came up here, and in four days' time you are going back home. After that you will never, I mean never, try to contact me again, do you hear me?'

Nodded.

'I'm sorry for what I did,' he said.

'You didn't do anything.'

'But I nearly did.' He looked away. 'I don't hit kids.' Did that mean he might hit men? 'I'd never hurt you, Danny. Let's just draw a line under it.' Stevie looked dead sad. 'I've been a total idiot. I should have told Megan. I mean, you could have turned up when we were married, you could have turned up any time. I just wish you'd told me you were coming.' Then he looked me dead in the eyes. 'In the few days we have left together let's try not to wind each other up. Deal?'

'Deal.'

Stevie put out his little hand. I shook it. Strong hand-shake for a skinny bloke.

Things were getting better and better. There was still a chance I could get what I came for.

'So what do you want to do today?'

'Have you got a football?'

'No, but the shops have.'

We grabbed our coats and went to a sports shop in Stevie's Mini. He went in and came back with a ball. Opened the car door and threw it to me. A white leather one, perfect.

'Ta,' I said, grinning.

Stevie drove to a park, and we walked across to a football pitch. Seeing as it was a school week there was nobody on it. Stevie grabbed the ball off me and kicked it a million miles up. I ran after it, got the ball at me feet. Game on. I looked back at Stevie, sitting on a bench. Game off.

I dribbled the ball over to him.

'Not playing?'

'No.'

Stevie knew how to punish me, buy a ball and then not kick it with me. I went over to the goal and practised penalties. Bit stupid doing that when there's no goalie. Even stupider when the nets aren't up. Took ages to get the ball back. Even with no goalie I still managed to miss a couple of spot kicks. How crap is that? Decided to practise corners. Again, a bit stupid with no one to aim at. I never get bored playing football, but I was getting bored now.

'Call that an in-swinger?'

Turned round. It was Stevie. I kicked the ball to him. Stevie flicked it up with his toes and did keepy-uppies – for ages. He must have done over fifty. Made my twenty-six look totally pathetic. I reckon he could do it all day if he wanted. Stevie was dead good, nothing like FB.

He ran off with the ball glued to his feet. Went after him, but I swear it took me ten minutes to get it off him, and when I did I think it's 'cos he let me. He did nutmegs, back-heels, step-overs, flick-ups, the works. It was like trying to get the ball off a magician.

'Okay, let's do some penalties,' he said.

The ground was a bit clarty, but I didn't mind. We decided to take fifty penalties each. I went in goal first. He scored thirty-seven. Reckon he could have got more but he was getting flash at the end doing trick shots and trying to score with back-heels. Then he went in. I only got nineteen, and I reckon he let some of those in. A couple of times he dived about five minutes after I'd kicked it.

'Howay, as you Geordies say, let's gan get some scran.'

Stevie picked up some sandwiches from a shop and drove us back to his flat. Was just about to open mine when Stevie's front-door buzzer went. Maybe it was Megan? Stevie put his sandwich down, walked over to a metal grille on the wall, and pressed a button.

'Hello.'

'Hi, Stevie, it's Connor.' Could tell from his face that this was not the visitor Stevie wanted. 'You okay?'

'Er, yeah,' mumbled Stevie.

'Well, if it's not contagious, can I come up?'

'Aye, of course,' he said, pressing a button. Then he turned to me. 'Danny, go and hide in my bedroom. Do not make a sound.'

Didn't know what was going on, but from Stevie's voice it was serious. I dashed into his bedroom and closed the door. A few seconds later I heard the front door open. Pressed me ear hard against the wood.

'Hello, Stevie,' said a voice that could only come from a big bloke.

'Hello, Uncle Connor.'

Guessed this must be the same uncle who took me dad in when he was a lad and stopped him being bad.

'What brings you here?'

'You. I went into the café. They said you were sick. Thought I'd come and see how you were.'

'Just a virus. Think I'm on the mend.'

'You must have got your appetite back, eating two packs of sandwiches.'

I'd left me cheese and tomato sandwich on the sofa.

'Yeah, feeling a bit peckish. I'll be okay by next week.'

'I hope you're not turning into a shirker.'

Stevie did a nervous laugh. 'No, I'm a grafter, Uncle Connor. You know me.'

'Oh, yes, I know you, Stevie.'

There was a long silence. The type that grown-ups like.

'You seem a bit tense, Stevie.'

'I'm fine.'

'Everything okay with you and Megan?'

I bet Stevie was squirming like a snake at that one.

'Yeah, she's just gone to see her ma for a few days.'

'If there was anything up, you'd tell me?'

'Of course. You're the only family I've got up here.'

Liar. Your son's in your bedroom.

'Do you want me to get you anything from the chemist?'

'No, I'll be okay.'

I did crossed fingers that they'd talk about the bad days. But me fingers weren't working.

'You playing football again?' said his uncle. He must have spotted the ball on the floor.

'Like to have a kick-about once in a while.'

'From the state of your shoes you've been having a kick-about this morning. Shouldn't be doing that if you're sick.'

Uncle Connor must have the same eyes as me mam.

'Just went in the park to clear my head.'

Heard a sigh. Don't know who it belonged to.

'If you need anything you know where to find me,' said Uncle Connor.

'Aye.'

'And lighten up, Stevie. You look like a condemned man.'

Twenty-Seven

•

The front door closed. The bedroom door opened.
It was Stevie, looking dead worried.

'What's wrong?'

'You are what's wrong. He knows I've got a kid.
Doesn't have to be Einstein to figure out he'd be
fourteen now. Same age as you. He'd want to know
what in God's name I was doing with my son back in
Scotland. He'd think I'd snatched you. He'd call the
police. Always said that if I did anything wrong again
he'd come down on me like a ton of bricks. He is not
a man you want to mess with. We're gonna have to
be careful.'

'Why?'

'Have you got sawdust for brains, Danny? Five minutes ago, I was a bloke with a fiancée, full stop. Now I'm wandering round Edinburgh with a teenage kid. If anyone notices they're gonna think, funny, he didn't have a kid last week, but he's got one now.'

Stevie was too afraid to go out, so we sat in and watched a movie. It was about a hit man in America being chased by the police. The hit man got caught and sent to the electric chair. Not exactly what you'd call a feel-good film. When it finished Stevie asked if I wanted some fish and chips.

'Aye,' I said. 'Can I come too?'

'No.'

'I've got to stay here all week?' I moaned.

Stevie had a think about me moan.

'Okay, you can come. But you stay in the car. And keep your wee head down.'

We parked in a street with tons of takeaways. Stevie went off to get the fish and chips, and I stayed in his Mini, bobble hat pulled down, peeping over the dashboard, like a spy.

He was coming out of the fish shop with his parcels when two drunks came swaying along the street, like a couple of FBs. As Stevie walked past, one of them, the fattest, grabbed one of his parcels. Even from right down the road I could hear Stevie screaming at them.

But the bloke wouldn't let go of the packet, holding it tight to his wobbly chest.

Stevie had nothing to hit them with. He was only armed with fish and chips. So he put the other parcel on a car roof, picked up a traffic cone and swung it at the fat bloke. The bloke was too paralytic to get out of the way, and it smacked him on the side of the head. It was only a traffic cone, but the bloke went down like he'd been demolished.

Stevie put the cone on the pavement, picked up both parcels and walked back towards the car as calm as you like. The other bloke just stood there, too drunk to know what to do next. Couldn't believe what I'd just seen. Me dad had just flattened a drunk with a traffic cone.

Stevie got in the car.

'Belter,' I said.

'Just a couple of bampots.'

Was dead proud of him for saving our chips. But more importantly, he'd done something else. He proved to me that he could take on FB.

After tea I washed the fish smell off me hands and sat next to Stevie on the sofa. Now that he'd had his tea and a beer it was the perfect time to tell him why I was really here. Was dead nervous, hands all clammy, even though I'd just dried them.

'Dad?'

He stared at me.

'Can you keep it to Stevie, please? That name freaks me out.'

Not a good start.

'Stevie.'

'What?'

'I've got something to tell you, about me mam.'

Stevie grabbed the TV remote. *The Simpsons* was on. He shut Homer up.

From his face Stevie looked like he knew bad stuff was coming.

'Is she sick?'

'Not sick.'

'Then what?'

Time to say it.

'In fact, it's not even about her, it's about her boyfriend.'

'Her boyfriend, what about her boyfriend?'

'He hits her.'

'Hits her?'

'Aye.'

'When?'

'Not all the time, but sometimes. When he's angry or she does something he doesn't like or he's been drinking. Any excuse, really.'

Stevie filled his cheeks with air and let it go.

'What's she done about it?'

'That's the problem, she's done nowt about it.'

'Where does this fella live?'

'In the room next door, with me mam.'

'Why doesn't she leave him?'

''Cos she loves him. They're going to get married.'

'Marrying the fella that batters her?'

Nodded.

'I'm sorry, Danny, really sorry. It must be hard for you.'

Too right.

'He's going to kill her.'

Stevie snorted. 'He won't.'

Why wasn't he taking me seriously?

'Two women get killed every week. It said so on the website. You've gotta read it. It's all there. It says mams who get hit don't do anything for ages. They think it'll get better. But it never does. Then they die.'

'Get her to read it.'

'She won't.' Me dad did a so-what shrug. 'You should see him. He choked me mam in Spain.'

'Danny, I'm sorry, but what in God's name are you telling me all this for?'

Paused, to get me words out proper.

''Cos I want you to sort it out.'

'Me?'

Now was the time.

'I want you to kill him.'

Stevie's eyes bulged like they were going to pop.

'You want *me* to kill your mam's boyfriend?'

Nodded.

Stevie laughed.

Then he went mental.

'This is the real reason you came up here?' he shouted, as he jumped up from the sofa.

'Aye.'

'You've got some cheek, Danny. I thought you'd come here to find your dad, make up for lost time, build bridges, but, no, you've just come to get me to do your dirty work for you.'

'I'm only little.'

'And I'm hardly King Kong. I weigh sixty-eight kilos.' Stevie flexed his biceps, but his muscles stayed hidden in his arms. 'I work in a café, Danny, I make sandwiches, pour teas, chop tomatoes, I'm not a hit man.'

'But you did bad stuff.'

'A long, long time ago. I didn't kill anyone,' said Stevie, putting the emphasis on the word 'kill'.

'Can't you just scare him away, then?'

'I'm not a bloody ghost either.'

Stevie walked round the room like the lion at the zoo, prowling, angry.

'He's a nasty bloke.'

'I've no doubt about that, plenty of them around. But I haven't seen your mam in years. I've got nothing to do with her. No disrespect, but she means nothing to me.'

He dragged his fingers through his hair. 'I don't owe your mam a thing.'

'But what about me?'

'What about you?'

'I'm not just somebody, I'm your son.'

Stevie got a pack of tabs from a drawer. Not seen him smoke before.

'Was trying to give these bastards up,' he said, fumbling with a box of matches. He got a flame, lit his tab and blew out a puff of smoke. The cloud drifted over me. I coughed, but he didn't seem to care, and just kept sucking on it, blowing more and more clouds. When the tab had gone he stubbed it out on a saucer and paced some more, like he hadn't done enough already.

'I've had it with all that stuff down there. I'm not going back, Danny, not even for you.'

Had an idea.

Got up and went to me coat, took the envelope out and handed it to him.

'What's this?'

'It's the money from the school trip I didn't go on.'

Stevie looked inside the envelope. 'And your mam gave you this?'

'No, her boyfriend did.'

'You want me to take the money your mam's boy-friend gave you, so I can kill him?'

Nodded.

'Danny, are you clinically insane?'

He threw the envelope on the sofa. I picked it up and gave it back to him, but he slapped me hand away. The envelope went flying. The money went all over the floor.

So that was it, not even a maybe, not even a perhaps, not even a 'Let me think about it, Danny', just a great big fat no. I'd come all this way for that. Might as well have gone on the trip with Amy. I felt tears knocking at the back of me eyeballs.

'Thought you'd help,' I cried, picking up the money. 'Thought dads always helped.' Shoved the money back in the envelope. 'The kids at school said that if their mam was in trouble their dad would sort it out. That's what I thought you'd do. That's what they said.'

'She'll be okay, Danny.'

'You don't know her, not like me. You don't know him, you don't know about domestic violence, you don't know anything. You just make sandwiches.'

Stevie looked like he'd been punched.

He finally came over and put a skinny arm round me.

'What you're asking for is too much,' he said, with his smoke breath. 'It's got nothing to do with me.'

'Could you sleep at night if you thought someone was hurting Megan?'

'I don't want to talk about this any more, Danny, do you hear me? It's finished.'

'But what…'

'I said the case is closed.'

Easy for him to close the case. He didn't have to go home, waiting for his mam to get bashed to death. He just had to wait for his girlfriend to come back. A lot easier.

'I'm off to bed,' said Stevie.

Wanted to cry again, but then I remembered I'd forgotten something. Me mam. Grabbed the phone from me bag and went in the hall.

Rang Mam's number. But Mam didn't answer. FB did.

'Hello,' he said.

Hung up dead quick.

Maybe it was too late. He'd already killed her.

Twenty-Eight

· ·

Me mam's always got her phone on her. Always. She loves that phone. He's killed her.

But before I could think what to do, me phone rang. Saw the name. It was her.

'Mam?'

'It's Callum.'

His voice made me freeze.

'Why did you hang up, Danny?' he said, sounding slurry.

'Want to speak to me mam.'

'So you don't want to speak to me, eh?'

''Course I do, I just, I just…' Just what? Think, Danny, think. 'I just thought you might be busy watching F1.'

He laughed.

'They don't have F1 mid-week.'

Wanted to hang up. But I couldn't. Not till I knew.

'Where's me mam?'

'You're wondering why I've got her phone, aren't you?'

Clenched a fist.

'Aren't you?' he went, getting angry.

'Aye.'

'She's got no one to call, so she gave it to me.'

'Where is she?'

'Said she wanted me to have it, 'cos she loves me so much.'

'Where is she, Callum?'

'The ringtone kept giving her a migraine.' And he laughed again.

'Please, tell me where she is.'

'Getting a bit anxious, General. Thought the country-side was meant to relax you.'

'Where is she?'

Silence.

Stood there listening to me heart, praying that another heart, one down in Gateshead, was still working. *Thump, thump, thump.*

Two women killed every week.

Me guts were screwed up tight like wrong-answer

paper. Could hardly breathe, like in the pool in Spain. What's he done to her?

Thump, thump, thump. Please, make her okay. *Thump, thump, thump.*

Please, God, make her okay, make her okay.

'Hello.'

'Mam?'

'Yes, what's up, Danny?'

'Has he hit you?'

'No, I'm fine.'

Me stomach unscrewed itself.

'Where is he?'

'In the kitchen, getting another lager.'

'Why did he have your phone?'

'I must have put it down.'

'Oh, Mam.'

'What did you say to him?'

Now it was her sounding scared.

'Nothing, Mam, just wanted to know where you were.'

'I was doing the ironing.'

'Why didn't he tell me that?'

'He was probably just having a joke.'

'He's the joke, Mam, a sick joke.'

'Please, let's talk about something else. Are you learning lots of stuff, Danny?'

Yeah, I've learned never to say 'Dad' in front of me dad's girlfriend when she doesn't know he's me dad, learned never to ask me dad to kill me mam's boyfriend, especially when he's angry with me for losing his girlfriend, learned never to go within a million miles of Scotland, and learned never to hang up when FB answers me mam's phone. That's what I'd learned.

'Aye, stuff,' I grunted.

'I think this experience will do you the world of good.'

Doubt that very much.

'I'd better get back to the ironing. You'll call me tomorrow night?'

''Course. Love you, Mam.'

'Love you too, Danny.'

I hung up, walked into the flat and put me phone away. Didn't want to watch telly so I switched off the light and curled up on the sofa. Couldn't even be bothered to take me clothes off. Just lay there, thinking. Me mountain of problems getting higher and higher.

Next morning I woke up and saw Stevie standing over me, holding a piece of toast.

'Fancy going to Edinburgh Castle?'

'Thought you didn't want to be seen with me,' I said, rubbing me eyes.

'True, but Edinburgh people don't go to Edinburgh Castle, it's for grockles.'

'Eh?'

'Tourists. Time I showed you a good old bit of Scottish history.'

Was that happy me mam was still alive, I'd have gone anywhere.

Stevie drove into Edinburgh, with me squidged down low. He parked and we walked up a long street made of bricks.

'The Royal Mile,' said Stevie.

'Why's it royal?'

'Because lots of kings and queens have been up this road. Not sure how many made it back down.'

I spotted a gadgie in a skirt with a massive fluffy black hat on his head wearing a tartan uniform and playing the bagpipes. You can't get more Scots than that. The bagpipes made the weirdest sound I'd ever heard in me life, but people must have liked it 'cos they kept putting money in his box. Unless they were paying him to stop.

'Does he know how to play it?' I said.

''Course he knows how to play it. He's a professional piper.'

'Sounds like he's squeezing a cat.'

'You're a numpty,' said Stevie. And to show that he must have liked the noise the gadgie was making he threw some coins in his box.

We walked into the castle and Stevie got some tickets. He was right about the grockles. Nobody here seemed to be from Scotland, just gibbering words that made no sense.

The castle was massive, with great thick walls and

loads of rooms full of old stuff. The best bit was the War Museum. Seemed like the Scots had been in loads of battles. Really must like fighting. Scraps all over the place, North America, Sweden, Germany, Africa, India. Stevie was turning Scots, I wonder why he didn't like fighting? It wasn't like I was asking him to go to war. All I wanted was him to kill one person.

Stevie looked sad when he was staring at the pictures of the soldiers who'd died. Maybe that's what he was worried about, that if he went into battle with FB, he'd die, and he'd never have a life, or get married to Megan, or buy his own sandwich shop.

We went outside and a gun went off. *Bang*. Got such a shock I jumped a mile in the air.

'It's the One O'Clock Gun,' said Stevie, laughing.

'What's that?'

'It used to tell ships the time.'

'Didn't they have watches?'

'Not in those days.'

'They'd tell them it was one o'clock by shooting at them?'

'Don't be daft, there's no shell in it.'

'So where are the ships they're firing at?' I said, looking out over Edinburgh at the sea.

'They aren't there any more.'

Firing a gun with no shell at ships that aren't there. I tell you, man, it's a strange place, Scotland.

Stevie seemed dead interested in all the stuff in the castle, the Crown Jewels, the army regiments, the canons, like he was proud of it. I'm not sure I'm that proud of anything in Gateshead. The Sage is quite cool, the Baltic's okay, and the Angel of the North's not bad, but apart from that it's just shops. You can't be proud of shops.

When I was standing next to the castle walls me phone went off. I wasn't expecting a call. I was scared something bad had happened at home. But it wasn't me mam, it was Amy.

'Hi, Danny.'

Didn't think just hearing a voice could make me so happy.

'How you doing, Amy?'

'Canny. How's your gran?'

'What gran? Oh, that gran, yeah, I think she's on the mend.'

'That's good.'

'I thought you weren't meant to use the phone unless it's an emergency.'

'This is an emergency. I wanted to speak to you.'

Grinned.

'What did you tell the teachers?'

'I told Mr Hetherington me mam was ill and I needed to call her.'

Seems Amy could be every bit as sneaky as me.

'Is Lanky Dave behaving hiself?' The silence said everything. 'What's he been doing?'

'Just the usual.'

I could picture that face, spitting out those words of his. I wished me arms were two hundred miles long and I could smack him right in the gob. Felt useless.

'Just tell him where to go, Amy, and if he does anything speak to the teachers.'

'I'm okay, Danny. Really, I'm okay.'

Amy had turned into me mam.

'I'll sort it when I get back,' I said.

'Get back? Where are you?'

'I mean, when you get back.'

'I don't want any more trouble, Danny. If you throw him down the stairs again you'll get expelled.'

'Leave it with me.'

'Please don't do anything silly, Danny. I'm fine. Anyway, I'm going to have to go now. We're going on a boat trip. Love you, Danny.'

'Love you too, Amy.'

Pause.

'You hang up first.'

'No, you.'

'Let's do it together. After three. One, two, three.'

Silence.

'You still there, Amy?'

'Aye.'

We both laughed.

'I'm really going, Danny.'

Click.

And this time she was gone.

Twenty-Nine

• •

Decided not to tell Stevie about the conversation I'd had with Amy. Knew what he'd say. Sort it out yourself.

After the castle we went up the coast and found a beach with a car park. The wind had dropped and the sea was as flat as a pancake. We grabbed some stones and did skimmers. I was the champion. Sixteen skims to ten.

'You've got a strong wee throwing arm,' he said.

Was good to get a compliment from him. Better than nothing, I suppose.

After doing skimmers we walked further up the beach and found a crazy golf course.

'Fancy a shot?' said Stevie.

'Why aye.'

We got two dodgy sticks, a scorecard and a couple of balls that looked like they'd been chewed by dogs. I'm not mad on golf, but we had a proper laugh. On hole number four Stevie hit the ball so hard it landed in the car park. I wasn't much better on number nine. Took me eight shots to get the ball in. Which dafty puts a hole on top of a hill? But I had me revenge on hole twelve, when Stevie took millions to get the ball in the Windmill. He hit the ball so hard it landed on the beach. I made him hit it all the way back to the hole.

'I need a sand iron for this,' he said, as he tried to putt the ball back across the beach.

Couldn't stop laughing.

We finished on the Dragon's Castle, a dead tricky hole where you had to get the ball down a tunnel and over a drawbridge. We both took tons of goes, but finally managed it. Stevie took the sticks and balls back. It started to drizzle, so we sheltered under the golf hut while Stevie totted up the scores.

'The result of the World Crazy Golf Tournament... Stevie – ninety-seven, Danny – eighty-three.'

'Well done,' I said, all grumpy like.

'What do you mean "well done", you stupid wee bampot? You won. The one with the lowest score in golf wins.'

'Get in,' I said, and did a little jig, like I'd seen a golfer do on telly.

I'd had a good day with Stevie. Just wished he'd do what I wanted. But I also wished something else. I wished Stevie hadn't got sent to Edinburgh and had stayed on Tyneside so I could see him any time I liked. He wouldn't be Stevie any more, he'd be me dad, me proper dad. That's what I wished.

As he drove back I had a question for him.

'Would you and me mam ever get back together?'

'There's more chance of the Pope supporting Rangers.'

No idea what that meant but guessed it was a no.

'Anyway, I've got Megan, and your mam's got a fiancé.'

'Who hits her.'

'Will you please stop talking about that nut-job? I am not going to do anything to him. Get her to speak to someone.'

He had no idea. She wouldn't even speak to me about it.

Decided not to waste any more words on it.

When we got back to Stevie's flat I called me mam. She answered straightaway. Which was good. But she was mortal. Which wasn't.

'How's my gorgeous Danny boy?'

'Alreet, Mam.'

'Love you. Wish I could give yus a massive greet big huggy hug.'

It was only half-seven. She must have been drinking from the minute she got in.

'Do you want to know what the weather's been like?' I said. Had the right paper open at the right page.

'Not really, Danny. Weather's even more boring than football.' Then me mam started hiccupping. 'Wash been happening?'

'Blow into a bag, Mam.'

'You're talking nonsense, Danny. You been drinkin' an all?'

Hated it when me mam got like this. Hated it even more knowing that FB was nearby, probably even more mortal.

Hiccup.

'Try and hold your breath, Mam.'

'I'm not at the baths, Danny. I hate swimming, me.'

'You've got the hiccups, Mam.'

Hiccup.

'Oh, yeah, so I have.'

Hiccup.

Then I heard something that made me bones shiver.

Slap.

'Mam, are you all right?' I shouted. 'Mam, what's happened?' The line had gone funny. Like she'd dropped the phone. 'Mam!'

'What did you do that for?' I heard me mam say.

Could hear FB's voice, but couldn't make out his words. Then she came back on.

'You still there, Danny?'

'Aye. Y'alreet, Mam? Did he hit you?'

'Yeah. Just needed to stop the hiccups.' But then I heard her choke back a sob. 'Why did he have to hit me that hard?'

Thirty

• • •

Thursday.

Last night's phone call with me mam had scared the cack out of me. To make things worse, in two days' time I was going to go back to the house where me mam's going to get killed. If only I'd got me dad to do what I wanted. The trip had been a total disaster. Everything had happened the wrong way round. I'd got rid of me dad's partner, but he wouldn't get rid of me mam's. Ironic or what? And I still hadn't come up with a way to sort out Lanky Dave. I was officially totally useless.

Got up. Had to. The sofa was starting to annoy me. Had a quick shower, then had me breakfast. Was on the last spoonful when Stevie appeared. He was on the phone, speaking all soft.

'Speak to you soon, sweetheart. Love you.'

Stevie switched his phone off, and whistled as he buttered his toast.

'Is Megan coming back?' I said.

'Might. I think the storm has passed.' And he started whistling again.

Glad someone was happy.

'What you fancy doing today, Geordie boy?'

'Don't care, it's your country.'

Think Stevie could tell I was hacked off.

'What's up?'

'He hit her.'

'Last night?'

'Aye. She had the hiccups.'

'A wee slap on the back's nee bother. We've all done it. He probably didn't mean to hurt her.'

'Aye, you're right. I'm sure when you hit Megan on the back she starts crying her head off. Nothing to worry about.'

Stevie looked away, like me words had drilled into his head and were defeating his words. *Nothing to do with me, Danny.*

He put his cheery face on. 'I don't get paid till tomorrow. How about doing the hills?'

Shrugged. Hills would be good. Then I'd be able to

tell me mam I'd walked up something, like I was meant to be doing.

Didn't say much on the way out of Edinburgh, but Stevie did. Hardly stopped, like he was trying to make up for the fact that he was never going to do what I needed him to.

We drove somewhere called the Pentland Hills Regional Park. Stevie stopped in a car park surrounded by trees. Behind the car park was a massive hill.

'We gannin all the way up there?'

'It's just a wee hill.'

Couldn't see anything wee about it. We got out of the car and started climbing. The path got steeper and steeper, and on some bits I was crawling on all fours like a bear.

'Where's the escalator?'

'Escalators are for wee bairns and grannies.'

I didn't talk the rest of the way up. Couldn't. The hill had taken all me spare breath away.

After absolutely ages we finally made it to the top. I was blowing like Adam Cooper in PE. Adam's the fattest kid in school.

'Here we are,' said Stevie, grinning. 'The top of Caerketton Hill. How's that for a view?'

Not really into views but had to admit this was quite a good one.

'Canny,' I went.

The wind was blowing like crazy up here. When you put your face into it, was like being slapped by invisible hands.

'You can see Edinburgh Castle, the Firth of Forth, and that big rock there is Arthur's Seat.'

'Who's Arthur?'

'Dunno, but whoever he was he must have had a massive backside.'

Could be funny could Stevie.

'Be great for sledging,' I said.

'Aye, the snow will be here soon enough.'

Spotted a pile of stones. Decided to take one. A wee souvenir, as me dad would say. Then we looked at the view. That was it. Not much else to do when you climb a hill, no shops, no football pitches, no cinemas, just view.

We went slowly back down, a stitch prodding me like I'd forgotten something. After loads of slips we came to a snowsports centre. It should have been called a carpet centre. Skiers were flying down the carpet on their skis.

'Can I have a shot?'

'I am not having you breaking your leg, not on my watch.'

Stevie could be quite strict, like some of me mates' dads. Considering he'd never really been a dad before he seemed to know what dads should do. I think he'd make a canny one if he put his mind to it.

After watching the skiers we went into a café. Never been to so many cafés in me life. Stevie bought me a can of pop and he had a coffee. We sat outside on a wooden bit sheltered from the wind. Then Stevie said something. Something I never expected him to say.

'I know it might sound strange, Danny, but part of me is glad you came. I sometimes wondered what you were like.'

'Honest?'

'Honest. Not often, but sometimes.' He paused. 'I never thought about your mam, but I sometimes thought about you.'

His words were the equivalent of a hug.

'So did you know anything about me?'

'Not much, but I knew your name.'

'How?'

'My sister told me. Not the name I'd have picked.'

'What's wrong with it?'

'Nothing. But if I had a son now I'd give him a good old Scottish name, like Frasier, or Malcolm, or Callum.'

Stevie could tell something was up. Me face told him.

'Y'okay, Danny?'

'Na, you said "Callum". That's what he's called, Callum Jeffries.'

Think Stevie realised he'd messed up. Now it was evens. I'd said 'Dad'. He'd said 'Callum'.

'Come on,' he said. 'Let's be heading back, I think it's going to rain.'

'Must be dead easy being a weatherman in Scotland,' I said. 'The weather forecast for the rest of the year – rain, goodnight.'

Stevie smiled. Then we ran to the car.

Had some good thoughts on the way back. Thought about what Stevie had said about him thinking about me. It made me feel good inside, like when me mind gets occupied by Amy.

About five o'clock when we got back. I took me phone outside to call me mam.

Worried as usual as the rings went.

'Hello.'

'Hi, Mam. Y'alreet?'

'Yes, I'm *alreet*,' she said, pointing out me Geordie.

'How's your back?'

'It's okay, Danny.'

Glad she was okay. Glad she wasn't mortal again. Glad she was still alive.

'Why were you drinking?'

'It's none of your business,' she snapped.

'What do you mean, none of me business?' I snapped back. 'You're me mam, aren't you?'

Silence.

'What did you do today?' she asked, but in the sort of voice a robot would have.

'You keep changing the subject, Mam. It doesn't matter what I did today. What matters is that he keeps on hitting you.'

Longer silence.

'I went for a walk by a lake, if you must know.'

'Is that it?'

'Then went for a walk up a wee hill.'

Wazzocks.

'Did you say "wee", Danny?'

Double wazzocks. Couldn't lie. She'd heard it.

'That's Scottish. Since when did you start talking Scottish?'

Come on brain, you useless lump.

'Erm, there's a Scots lad in our class. Must have got it off him.'

'Who's that, then?'

Triple wazzocks.

'He's new. Can't remember his name.'

Stupid words. Just keep dropping me in it.

'So what are you doing tomorrow?' she said.

Quadruple wazzocks.

Why did I tell me mam I'd call her every night? Each time I ring her something goes wrong.

'Not sure.'

Silence.

'Is that all Mr Chatterbox has got to say?'

'Aye.'

'Well, goodnight, Danny, sleep well.'

'Aye, you too.'

Mam hung up.

It was the first time that week she hadn't said, 'Love you'. I was doing this for her, and all she could do was pick on me words. There was a stack of dustbins by the front door. I kicked them over. Then I picked up a dustbin lid and threw it. It hit a car in the street, and set the alarm off.

Ran back in the house, slammed the door and raced up the stairs to Stevie's flat. Slammed that door too.

Puff, puff, puff.

Stevie was sitting with a cup of tea.

'Y'okay?'

He'd seen me hot face, me breath coming out fast.

'Aye, just perfect.'

I was now officially the world's biggest liar.

Thirty-One

• •

'**Last day today**, Danny,' said Stevie. 'Let's make it a good one, eh?'

He took me go-karting. The track was miles out of Edinburgh. Guess Stevie was still scared about Uncle Connor and being seen with me. Wouldn't have to worry about that for much longer.

There weren't many people at the go-kart track, less people to crash into. Stevie was good at the go-karts. I wasn't. Didn't like going fast. Reminded me of FB, pressing his fat foot to the floor.

'Enjoy that?' said Stevie, when we'd parked our karts.

'Not bad.'

Took me smelly helmet off and put it on a table.

'You've got to learn to accelerate out of the corners.'

'Whatever.'

Think he could tell I was still hacked off. Next week he was going back to sandwiches. I was going back to a school with a bully who's messing with me girlfriend, and a house where me mam gets hit by the bloke she's going to marry. If it wasn't for Amy wouldn't be much point in going back at all.

We got in his Mini. But he didn't start it. Went dead quiet for a bit, like in an exam.

'Danny…'

'What?'

'… when you're older, maybe you can come back up and see me.'

'How much older?'

Stevie squirmed in his seat. 'Don't know, maybe eighteen.'

'Why eighteen?'

'It'll work out better, then.'

'Why?'

'It just will.'

'But that's over three years away.'

'It's not that long.'

'It's over three years.'

Stevie leaned over the steering wheel and said the rest in whispers. 'Danny, I can't let you stay here, and I can't go back to Gateshead. That's the way it is. You're just going to have to wait.'

'Fair enough.'

'No, it's not fair enough,' he said. 'I'd love to do something to help you, I really would. But I can't, not the thing you want. I mean, imagine you were me. What would you do?'

'Kill him.'

Stevie shot out a quick laugh.

'You've got no job, no responsibilities, no idea what the repercussions could be. The answer's no.'

Knew that. No need to keep saying it.

'Can we go now?'

But before we left he leaned across again and grabbed me hand.

'There's something else I'd like you to know.'

No idea what was coming next, and from the look on his face neither did he.

'I've not given you much thought all these years,' he said, 'but after this week, I'll not be able to stop thinking about you.'

He looked at me as he smiled.

His eyes were brown. The same as mine.

Thirty-Two

•

I was dead careful on the phone to me mam that night. Didn't do a 'wee' or anything. Got me reward.

'Love you, Danny.'

'Love you too, Mam.'

Me mam wasn't mortal drunk, and didn't sound terrified. She sounded normal. I was happy. But the happy didn't last, because one second later she dropped her nuclear bomb.

'We'll pick you up from school the morrow.'

Me tongue was in knots.

'N-n-no, it's okay, Mam. I'll make me own way back.'

'Don't be silly,' she said. 'It's only down the road. We'll pick you up.'

'But…'

'No buts, Danny, we didn't get to see you go, at least we can be there when you arrive. See you at one.'

She hung up.

Oh, man.

Sat on the stairs outside Stevie's flat and had a long think. But like most of me thinks it didn't turn into anything useful.

Trudged back inside.

'Is your mam okay?' said Stevie, when he spotted me sulky face.

'Aye, seems to be.'

Told Stevie about me other problem.

'That's an easy one to fix,' he said. 'You just get yourself an early train. Arrive before the coach, go and hide somewhere in the school, and when the coach drops everyone off, just join the crowds.'

Me face lit up like a bonfire.

'Belter.'

I gave Stevie a hug. He squeezed me back.

He grabbed his coat, went out and got us pie and chips. Didn't get into a scrap this time.

'Won't your mam find out you've not been on your trip?' said Stevie, dropping a long, gangly chip in his gob.

'Not if I'm smart.'

'Sneaky must be your middle name.'

That was me all right. Danny Sneaky Croft.

After a bit Stevie stopped eating chips and shuffled over. He put an arm around me. It should have felt weird, but it didn't. It felt good.

'This week's been a test for us, that's for sure,' he said. 'Do you think we passed?'

'Aye, I think we passed.'

Turned to him. 'Will you write to me?'

Stevie heaved out pie breath. 'Can't, you know that.'

'I could email you, then delete it.'

'No.'

Thought I'd better change the subject.

'Have you heard from Megan?'

'Aye, we're going to meet up on Saturday night.'

'Good.'

'More like brilliant.'

Finally, he moved towards me. I thought he was going to hug me again. But what he did was even better. He said two words.

'Night, son.'

Thirty-Three

•

Didn't sleep much that night, me brain going haywire, as if maths, English and French were all attacking it at once.

It had taken every bit of sneakiness I had to find me dad, but now I'd found him I wouldn't get to see him again for years. It didn't seem fair, like getting a birthday present, then having it swiped off you for no reason. But at least I'd tracked him down. Felt like a blank space in me life had been filled in. I was like the other kids in class. Had a mam and a dad. Proud of meself for doing that.

Proud of meself for something else as well. In the

night I'd come up with a way to deal with the Lanky Dave problem. In the morning I asked Stevie if he had a picture of his Uncle Connor.

'What do you want a picture of him for?'

'Just do.'

Stevie went in his room and came back with an old photo.

'It's not very recent.'

It showed Uncle Connor in his shorts, muscles bulging.

'Perfect,' I said, and put it in me bag.

'And I've got a wee present for you.'

Stevie went in the kitchen, came back with the ball, and threw it to me.

'Cheers.'

'Time to go, Geordie lad.'

I stuffed the ball in me sports bag, grabbed me coat, and went down the stairs for the last time. We got in Stevie's Mini and headed off. It was raining again, the wipers *swish swoshing* across the windscreen. Apart from that and the engine we had silence. Wished he'd turn the radio on. Silence can be horrible, even worse than noise.

We were halfway round a roundabout when Stevie finally asked a question. 'Are you glad you came, Danny?'

Not a hard question, but hard enough.

'Sort of.'

Glad to have found me dad, but not glad about what had happened with Megan, and the thing that didn't happen.

'Are you glad I came?'

'Sort of,' he said. Then a little smile cracked his face. 'Yeah, I'm glad you came.'

The silence returned. The way it does.

That's the last thing either of us said, all the way to the station. Me gran would have been ashamed of me. But now the silence seemed right. Think we'd said everything that needed to be said.

He stopped in a car park and I got me bag out of the boot.

'Walk you to the train?' Nodded. 'Have you got your ticket?' Nodded again. I knew about singles and returns now. Not that I'd be coming back here, not for years.

We went into the station and Stevie checked the departure board.

'There's a train to Newcastle in ten minutes. Plenty of time to get you back before your coach.'

We walked slowly to the platform, like we didn't want to get there. The train was already in. Then I saw something I wish I hadn't, a young lass and an older bloke. Except these two weren't rowing or fighting, they were holding each other tight, like me and Amy when no one's around. It set me off again, like the picture at Aunty Tina's.

Stevie put his skinny arms around me again. But that only made it worse.

'Come on, Danny, everything will be okay.'

'No, it won't,' I sniffed. 'You've no idea what it's like. He'll keep hitting her, then he'll kill her, like they said on the website. Then I'll be on me own.'

'That's not going to happen,' he said, his stern voice on. 'If he does something again, call the police, just call them.'

'Two mams get murdered every week. Where were the police then?'

Stevie took his arms back and shook his head. I looked up at him. 'Please help me, Dad.'

'Oh, heavens above.'

He bent down so our eyes were on the same level, and took hold of me hands. I could tell other people were looking, wondering what was going on, but for once I couldn't care less.

'Danny, you came up all this way on your own. You're a strong laddie, a clever laddie, now you've got to be a brave laddie. Please, I'm asking you, be strong, Danny, for yourself, for your mam.'

'It's not just about me mam, it's about you.'

He pulled me head into his chest. And the tears came again.

'The train for London Kings Cross will shortly be leaving from Platform Seven,' said a voice from somewhere.

Stevie squeezed me hard. But it was different to the squeezes that me gran and Aunty Tina gave me. It was a draw between feeling happy and sad. I didn't want it to ever stop. I wanted to stay squeezed for ever. Couldn't. The train was going to leave.

Stevie let go. I wiped me tears on me coat. Stevie wiped his eyes on his sleeve. He took a fiver from his wallet and stuffed it in me pocket. I hate it when FB does that. Didn't hate me dad doing it.

'Be strong, wee fella.'

Never felt weaker.

Needed to go.

'Bye, Dad.'

I picked up me bag and got on the train. It was packed. Didn't want to see me dad on the platform, looking sad, so I just sat down on the floor by the toilets, like I'd done last Sunday. The door closed. Then I heard a whistle. The train started moving, slowly, slowly, then faster and faster and faster. The sky flew past. Edinburgh was gone.

Thirty-Four

• •

The train tanked along, clouds whizzing by like fluffy racehorses.

It stopped at Dunbar, a place I'd never heard of, then it started again, and then, for no reason at all, it slowed right down and stopped. Got up and looked out of the window. We weren't at a station, we weren't at a town, we were next to a field. Don't catch many trains, but even I know they don't pick people up from fields.

A Scotsman's voice came on.

'Sorry for the delay, ladies and gentlemen, but we have a faulty train ahead of us. I'll report back when I have further details.'

Looked at me watch. It was 10.22 a.m., still bags of time to get back before the coach. Sat down again, wondering how Amy was. I wanted to call her, but I'd forgotten to charge me phone. I hoped she wasn't getting any grief from Lanky Dave. Even if he was annoying her, I had a plan to deal with him now. One that would make him stay away for ever.

The wait went on and on. Looked at me watch. 10.51 a.m. It was like sitting on the wall watching me dad's front door. I stood up and looked out of the window again. Cows were bending down, eating. Watching them made me feel hungry. I should have bought a chocolate bar or something. Not like I didn't have enough money. I saw people walking past with bags of food. Thought about getting some, but changed me mind. I didn't want to lose me spot, or have someone nick me bag, and me football.

Wondered where we were. When we flew to Spain they had a map with a little plane on it to show you how far you'd gone. Trains should do that. All I knew was that this train wasn't going anywhere. I started having bad thoughts. What if the coach got back to school before me? Mam would find out I wasn't on it. She'd think I'd run away and call the police. Wouldn't that be just typical? Mam wouldn't do it for her, but she'd do it for me.

The Scots bloke came on again.

'We're sorry for the delay, ladies and gentlemen—' Just tell us why we're not moving. I didn't buy a ticket to look at cows – 'The train in front has suffered a malfunction...'

First it was faulty now it's suffered a malfunction, a posh word for knackered. As if enough hadn't happened this week, now this. I could borrow someone else's phone and ring me mam, but what would I tell her? I'm stuck on a train? From the Lake District, she'd say, all surprised. When did they build that line?

I punched the toilet door in frustration.

'Oi,' came a voice from inside. Knowing my luck a massive Scotsman would come out and punch me right back.

I got up and walked about in me small space. No one else seemed that bothered we weren't going anywhere, just buying food, talking, drinking, listening to music. I guess none of them had lied to their mams, none of them were coming back from where they shouldn't be, none of them were about to get the rollocking of their lives.

The train stayed stopped.

Just when I thought I was going to spend the rest of me life next to a cow field, I felt the train budge. A cheer went up in the carriage. The train moved, then it got faster and faster, but still not as fast as me heart, which was now going mental.

I could hardly bear to look at me watch. But had to.
12.02 p.m.

Wazzocks.

'Do you know how long till we get to Newcastle?'
I said to a bloke sitting on the floor with a can.

'About an hour,' he said, a beery smile on his face.
Wish I had something to smile about. 'Late for something?' he went, slurping his beer.

'Aye.'

'The match?'

Didn't even know if the Toon were playing at home
today. How bad is that?

'Don't go to any matches.'

'Don't blame you.'

I didn't want to talk to the bloke. I'd had it with
drunks, had it with everything. I was never going to get
to school in time. I went through in me head what I'd
tell me mam. *I didn't fancy the Lakes, so I went to Scotland.
Where in Scotland?* she'd ask. *Edinburgh.* And then she'd
know. *That's where your dad lives,* she'd say. *That's why you
went there, isn't it?* I'd nod. Then she'd make me tell her
why and things would be even worse in our house than
they are now, expect I'd be the one that gets screamed
at, and me mam would make sure I never saw me dad
again, not even when I was eighteen.

I started to pray to Amy's God that our train would
break down, that I'd never get home. But it's funny, just

when you want a bad thing to happen it never does. The train just seemed to get faster and faster and faster.

The speaker bloke was off again.

'Next stop: Newcastle. Next stop: Newcastle.'

Okay, heard you first time Mr Scotsman.

I stood up and looked out, saw houses, Geordie houses. I never thought I'd hate coming back to Tyneside, but I did now. I tried to spot St James' Park. I thought if I saw that it might bring me good luck, but, no, too many buildings in the way.

Looked at me watch again. 1.06 p.m. The coach would be there now, the kids all getting off, laughing, pushing, grabbing their bags. Amy would be there too, hugging her mam and dad, but me mam and FB wouldn't be hugging anyone. They'd be wandering around looking for me, not finding me.

'Danny, has anyone seen Danny?' me mam would shout in her scared voice.

'Danny?' Mr Hetherington would say, confused. 'He's not here.'

'What do you mean he's not here?'

'He didn't come on the trip. He told me he was going to his gran's.'

Me mam's face would go a weird colour, then she'd have to sit down, then she'd call me gran and find out I wasn't there, then she'd call the police, then I'd turn up, then she'd be happy, for one second, then she'd go mental, for about a million seconds, then she'd get FB to batter me, then me mam would batter me. That's what would happen.

Felt like I wanted to puke.

The train stopped. Picked up me bag and moved to the door.

'See you, Geordie,' said the bloke with the can.

Said nothing. Just got off the train with me bag and trudged across the Central Station. I didn't even bother running. What was the point? Too late for that. I checked me envelope. Still had over a hundred quid, more than enough to get the train back to Edinburgh. But just another stupid idea, from the king of stupid ideas.

Went to the taxi rank.

'Where to, kidda?' said the taxi driver.

Good to hear a Geordie voice again.

Thought of getting him to take me straight to school, but changed me mind.

They'd have gone by now. Told him me address in Whickham.

I didn't want to talk. But he did.

'Where've yous been?'

Sigh.

'Scotland.'

'With the Sweaties?' Thought I got Geordie, but had no idea what he was on about. 'Y'on your own?' he went, his eyes watching me in his mirror.

Nodded.

'Long way to gan on your tod. Been seeing your folks?'

Never thought I'd hear meself say it, but I did.

'Aye, been seeing me dad.'

'Canny time?'

'Aye, canny.'

Which for once was nearly the truth.

The driver stopped talking after this. He must have known he wasn't going to get much out of me.

We crossed the Tyne and ten minutes later pulled into FB's street.

'Here you are, bonny lad.'

Looked at FB's drive. His car was gone. They must still be at the school, looking, waiting, wondering. Me mam would be on her phone to me, not getting through to me, trying to figure out what was going on. I thought about getting out, and waiting for them to come back, but that might make me mam even madder.

'Can we gan somewhere else, please?'

'Aye, long as it's not Scotland.'

Asked him to take me to me school.

'It's shut. It's Saturday.'

'Just take me, will you?'

He shrugged his shoulders. 'It's your money, kidda.'

I thought the journey from Edinburgh was the worst I'd ever been on. Wrong, this one was, 'cos this was taking me to me mam and him. I said another little prayer in me head. I prayed to the God of Miracles to save me.

A few minutes later the driver turned the corner where the school was. I closed me eyes. I knew what I'd see when I opened them. One car, Range Rover, two people standing next to it, biting nails, looking up and down the street for the lad who never got off the bus.

'Here you gan,' said the driver. 'Looks like you've got a welcome committee.'

I snapped me eyes open. Couldn't believe what they were telling me. On both sides of the road were cars, and next to the cars were loads of people. I rubbed them in case it was a dream, but it wasn't, it was real life. No sign of the coaches, just tons of mams and dads.

'This alreet for you?' he went, slowing down.

I didn't want him to drop me right next to me mam and FB.

'Na, keep gannin.'

Just like in Edinburgh I slumped in the seat, with me eyes peeking over the top. Then I spotted them. I saw FB first, couldn't miss him, not with that belly, then I saw me mam, on her phone.

'Can you gan a bit further, mate?'

I squidged right down so they wouldn't see me as we went past. A few seconds later, I got up and looked back. FB was smaller now, me mam was the size of a fingernail. Safe enough.

'You can stop here.'

He did.

'Cheers.'

Paid the fare and gave him a tip. Seen me mam do that. It's what you have to do unless you want them to swear at you. Grabbed me bag and got out.

'Take care, kidda.'

Too right I will.

The taxi drove off, and I went up to a mam and dad, standing by a car that looked like it was held together by rust.

'What's gannin on?'

'Divvent knaa,' said the woman, sucking on a tab. She was surrounded by smoke, like she was on fire.

'The bus must be knackered,' said the dad. 'Shoulda been here ages ago.'

Yes. Yes. Yes.

It was like scoring the winning goal for Newcastle in the Champions League Final, only better. The first bit of good news I'd had for ages. The train had been late, but the coach was even later. Me mam and FB would think I was still stuck on it. I wasn't in the clear yet though, I needed to look like I'd been on the trip. If they saw me walking down the street with me bag they'd wonder how I'd got back before the coach. I'm a fast runner, but not that fast.

The coaches usually stop in the school playground,

next to the main entrance. I needed to make it look like that's where I was coming from. Decided to do a massive loop round the school grounds. Walked down the street and through the hole in the fence that Year Ten cut, across the football pitch at the back of the school, and round the side by the burned science lab. Then I found a spot by the metal dustbins where I could wait.

Didn't have to wait long. Twenty minutes later the coaches turned up. Just as I thought, they drove into the car park and stopped right in front of the school. A few seconds later they all started to pour off. Time to make me move. I grabbed me bag and walked along the side of the buses, where I couldn't be seen from the road. Lads and lasses were dashing down the steps. I hurried forward to join the crowd. I'd only gone two steps when a hand touched me shoulder.

'Danny?'

Turned.

It was Amy, looking all rosy from being outside all week.

Me mouth was short of words. All I could think to say was, 'Hi.'

'What you doing here?'

'I, um, just wanted to welcome you back.'

'That's so thoughtful of you, Danny. What's the bag for?' she said, looking down.

Thought quick. Should have thought slow.

'I've been shopping.'

Amy gave me a strange look.

'Shopping? You hate shopping.'

'Just getting a few things for me mam.'

'How's your gran?'

'Gran? Oh, a lot, lot better. Almost totally cured.'

Amy inched her toes forward, like she was desperate for a hug. I wanted to grab her so much. But I couldn't. Not in school.

'So how were things with you-know-who?' I asked.

She looked across the playground at the lumbering figure of Lanky Dave, who had a kid in a headlock.

'He's been a total idiot. I'll give you a full report, but not now.' Amy quickly touched my hand. 'Me mam and dad have been waiting ages. I'll call you later.'

'Aye, ta-ra, Amy.'

'Love you,' she mouthed.

'Love you too.'

Amy hurried away.

I walked quickly towards the road, hoping no one else came to ask where I'd been or what on earth I was doing at school on a Saturday.

Nobody did.

Me mam spotted me first. She hurried across the road, wearing a big grin. She got close. I checked her face for marks, but couldn't see anything. She'd probably put make-up on.

'Oh, Danny.' She gave me a hug. Not as big as Stevie's, but still a good one. 'I've missed you,' she went.

'Aye, me too.'

The squeezing stopped, then FB waddled up, smiling, of course, and rubbed me hair with his fat hands.

'Good trip, General?'

Stop General-ising me.

'Aye, not bad.'

FB shoved a couple of quid in me coat pocket. God, I was minted.

'What's that, Danny?' said me mam.

'What's what?'

Mam reached into me shirt pocket and pulled out the Scottish five-pound note. She looked at it and then back at me.

'Found it, in the street.'

'A Scottish note, in the Lake District?'

'Yeah,' said FB. 'You get a load of Jocks in the Lakes coming back from Blackpool. They've probably sent a search party from Glasgow to look for it.'

Me mam put the note back in me pocket, but she wasn't finished yet. 'So how come you're so late back?'

'Bus broke.'

'Why didn't you call me? We've been waiting ages.'

'Me phone was out of juice.'

Probably the only truthful thing I'd told her all week.

Me mam asked a few more questions on the way home, but not too many, and not too hard. I guess she'd been quizzing me every night. I had another closer look at her face, but I couldn't see anything. I reckoned if he'd battered her on Tuesday, the marks might have gone by now. I sniffed the air. Couldn't smell beer or TCP either. She probably had a massive bruise where he'd belted her on the back. But I'd never see that. Just glad me mam had survived the week.

FB drove fast, but no one made him go radgy. He parked in front of his garage and we went in the house. I went upstairs and crashed on me bed. Took the ball out of me bag and hugged it tight, like a keeper at a corner. It made me feel good.

The door opened and me mam came in and sat on the bed next to me. She looked at the ball.

'Is that a new one?'

'Aye, got it from a shop.'

'You've got a ball.'

'Fancied another one.'

'Looks expensive.'

'Wasn't that much,' I said, even though I hadn't a clue.

'Are you all right, Danny?'

'Aye.'

'You didn't sound fine on the phone. You sounded distant.'

'I was distant.'

'You know what I mean.' She scrabbled her nails on the duvet. 'We're working things out.'

'He hit you when you were on the phone. He made you cry.'

'Look, Callum gets worked up when I've done something wrong.'

'Hiccupping's not wrong.'

'He was trying to stop them.'

I looked away. For the first time ever I felt ashamed of her. I thought she was the best mam on the planet. I thought she was clever. I thought she always did the right thing. But I was wrong. She just wanted me to agree with her. Yes, Mam, no, Mam, three bags full, Mam. But I wasn't going to. Was never going to. Because I knew what she didn't. I knew the facts. The facts she wouldn't even look at.

She got up and walked to the door.

'You didn't send us a postcard.'

Greetings from Edinburgh. That would have made her choke on her cereal.

'No, Mam, I didn't.'

Thirty-Five

•

I rang Amy that night to find out what the score was with Lanky Dave.

Not good.

'He tried to sit next to me every time we got on the coach, tried to kiss me, touched me when the teachers weren't looking. Just a massive pain in the butt.'

'Why didn't you tell the teachers?'

'I can deal with it, Danny.'

Nobody wants help any more.

'Amy.'

'I'm going to avoid him.'

'He's in our class.'

'I'll give him an ultimatum. If he does anything really bad I'll go to Mrs Brighton.'

'Why not ask your dad to do something?'

'What? Threaten a fourteen-year-old kid?'

'No, threaten the fourteen-year-old kid's dad.'

'That's how wars start.'

'Well, if you won't do anything, I will.'

'Please don't do anything stupid, Danny.'

'Me, do anything stupid? As if.'

Didn't think it was possible for Amy to annoy me, but she had. Just like everyone else she didn't want to hear what I had to say. Like all me words were worthless.

But at least I had something new to take me mind off things – Scotland. Thought about all the things I liked about it – me dad, crazy golf, fish and chips, skimming stones, cafés, the lions, the castle, kick-about. Thought of all the things I hated about it – rain, funny voices, go-karts, slow trains, steep hills, Scottish football, lumpy sofas. Eight–seven. Not a bad result.

But of all the things in Scotland, the thing I thought about most was me dad. I'd be eighteen next time I saw him, and he'd be thirty-four. He'd probably have a big belly, and no hair, and hairy ears like the dads at school. I'd be different too – bigger, maybe have a job, and a tash, and a tattoo of Amy on me arm. But me mam wouldn't be around. And FB would be in prison for murder.

At school on Monday I heard loads more about the trip, so if me mam quizzed me, I'd have all the right answers.

The stories, in the order I heard them:

Stuart Martin and Colin Duffin had a fight over a missing packet of crisps. Stuart said that Colin had nicked them and Colin said he never. They had a punch-up in the toilet and Stuart swallowed a tooth. The teachers broke it up. But ten minutes later Stuart found the crisps at the bottom of his bag. Mr Tobin made him apologise.

Barry told me about Jamie Cavendish falling in a lake. Jamie's a massive show-off. There was a rock far out, and a bunch of lads bet him a fiver he couldn't jump across to it. Jamie said he could. He took a huge run-up, like in the Olympics, and missed the rock by a mile. Barry reckoned they were still laughing an hour later.

Tony Heskill was caught with his hand up Michelle Arthur's sweatshirt. Michelle said that she had an itch that needed scratching. Mr Pensford said that he'd have accepted this explanation if the itch was on her back. They both got detention.

Up one of the hills Kevin Nyland stopped to have a pee off a rock. The rock was wet, and Kevin slipped, mid-pee. He wet his pants, sprained his ankle and broke his wrist. Shame nobody had a phone to get it on film. If they had it would have got a billion hits.

Jason Glenorchy and Heidi Rhodes sneaked out one night. Jason said they went all the way. Heidi said they never. So they probably did.

Those were the main stories. Other things:

No one got much sleep because of farting, snoring, shuffling, talking. It was freezing cold, the trips were mega-boring, and Mrs Peck, the geography teacher, talked about glaciers and stuff, but no one could remember what she said.

Now it was time to talk to Lanky Dave. I saw him swaggering across the playground during break.

'Oi, Dave,' I shouted.

He stopped, turned and walked back to me, arms hanging like a gorilla's.

'What do you want, Croft?'

'I want you to leave Amy alone.'

'I want you to leave Amy alone,' he said, like he was on helium. Then he put his face up close to mine. 'You're wasting your breath. She let me do things you could never dream about.'

'Not what she told me,' I said, trying with all me might to stop me voice from cracking. 'If you don't leave her alone, I'm going to get this bloke to sort you out.'

With a shaky hand I took the photo of Uncle Connor from me pocket and handed it to Lanky Dave.

He stared at the picture. 'Who's that fat bastard?'

'He's not fat, those are muscles. Me Uncle Connor is a boxing champion, from South Shields.'

I didn't want Big Dave to know that Uncle Connor lived in Edinburgh, and he wasn't even me uncle.

An evil grin spread like an oil slick across Lanky Dave's face.

'I couldn't give a flying fart about your boxing kangaroo uncle. My brother's in the army. He's a black belt in karate.'

Lanky Dave tore the photo of Uncle Connor into lots of tiny pieces, and walked away, laughing.

Thirty-Six

. . .

Me mam didn't ask any more questions about the trip. Typical. Just like in class, when you know the answer they never ask you, when you don't know, they do. I guess she was fed up of talking to me, 'cos I'd always end up asking her the same questions, and she'd always come up with the same stupid answers.

But there was one thing she never stopped talking about. The wedding.

'Danny, we'd like you to be a pageboy.'

'What's that mean?'

'It means you'll be the boy who carries the wedding rings down the aisle on a little pillow,' said FB, butting in.

I could tell from their faces it was a big deal for them, but for me it was the smallest deal in the world. It was just wrong. She won't marry the bloke she has a baby with, but she will marry the bloke she's had no baby with, and who batters her. Mad.

'No,' I said.

'Danny,' said me mam, in her finger-pointing voice. 'We're giving you a wonderful opportunity to take part in our wedding.'

'I'd rather just watch.'

Then I ran up to me room.

'Danny,' screamed me mam.

She didn't follow me upstairs. Neither did FB. Think they knew that nothing in the world would make me carry their stupid rings on a stupid pillow.

But me mam wasn't me only problem.

Amy and me went to McDonald's one night after school.

'What's up, Danny?' she said, taking me hand.

'You need to tell the teachers about Lanky Dave.'

Amy took her hand back.

'How many times do I have to tell you? I can handle it.'

'But what if he picks on someone who can't handle it, eh? And they gan and top themselves.'

'Can we change the subject?'

'No, I'm not going to change the subject, Amy.

Problems divvent solve themselves. We've got an anti-bullying policy at school.'

'It's not bullying. He's just being irritating.'

'Yeah, and that's how it starts.'

'How what starts?'

Hadn't wanted to tell Amy. Not ever. But I didn't want what happened to me mam to happen to her. I needed her to know what you get when you do nothing.

'Domestic violence.'

'What are you talking about, Danny?'

Was time to tell her.

Three, two, one.

'Callum hits me mam.'

Amy put her burger down, and stared at me, open-mouthed.

'Hits her? How? Why? When?'

All the same questions that had been destroying me brain for months and months. I didn't hold back. Told her every single thing he'd done to me mam.

Didn't think it was possible to look shocked, confused and sad at the same time, but Amy's face managed it. She pushed her burger away.

'That's terrible, Danny,' she said. 'That's so terrible. I'm really sorry for you. It must be horrible.'

'Worse than that.'

And then she put her quizzical face on.

'The school trip?'

'What about it?' I said, swallowing spit.

'I know what you did.'

She must be a mind reader, like me mam.

'You didn't stay behind because of your gran, did you?'

Shook me head. Me secret was out.

'You stayed back to make sure your mam was okay.'

And then she leaned over the cold burger and gave me a kiss on the lips.

'I'm so proud of you, Danny.'

Thirty-Seven

• •

Amy and me agreed to meet in a couple of days to figure out what to do next. She promised not to talk to anyone about it until we'd come up with a plan.

I felt better having told her. But even though Amy's dead clever, I didn't think she'd solve anything. I mean, me mam wasn't just putting up with FB, she was going to marry him, as if the wedding would somehow solve everything, and the ring would stop her getting battered. Like it would give her magic powers.

Blah, wedding, blah, wedding, blah. It was the only thing me mam seemed interested in. She'd even cut back on the chocolate biscuits so she didn't look quite so big on her big day. Tried to look as bored as I could when she talked about it, but it didn't stop her. *Which bag do you think looks best? Do you think veil or no veil? Which song shall I walk down the aisle to?* She just went on and on and on, like an F1 car, one that never ever runs out of petrol.

We went to look at the church, a horrible black building near Blaydon. It was freezing inside, old wooden benches, smelled of damp. But Mam and FB smiled like they'd died and gone to heaven. Then we went to a golf club, where the wedding reception would be. Place was warmer, but still a bit of a dump. FB seemed happy with it. It had a big bar.

Me mam and me put some Christmas lights up outside the house. FB came back from the pub and tore them down.

'I'm not having my house look like some grotty grotto,' he steamed.

Me mam didn't even bother to argue with him. Like she'd given up. But I hadn't.

'Why did you tear the lights down?'

''Cos they're tacky. When you pay the mortgage, you can put up as many lights as you like, General.'

FB opened another can.

'So what do you want to be when you grow up?'

Miles from you.

'Dunno.'

'Danny,' moaned me mam, who was ironing one of his giant shirts.

Weird. You get shouted at school for talking, you get shouted at home for not talking.

'Footballer,' I said.

'Earn a lot of money, those boys, millions for kicking a lump of leather. Still, you could look after us. Buy me a Ferrari and buy your mum a running machine to shift all that meat off her.'

FB laughed, as though it was funny. Me mam just carried on ironing. Like she'd gone as deaf as me gran.

'You can talk,' I said, staring at him.

FB put his can down and glared back at me, face reddening.

'Maybe you'd be better off taking up boxing if you're going to come out with stuff like that.'

'Gonna hit me as well, are you?'

Callum looked like he was about to explode.

'Danny, go to your room,' said me mam.

Didn't need to be asked twice. Ran up to me room, and looked out at the street. Saw all the other houses with their twinkly decorations. Ours the only one without a single Christmas light. This was how it was going to be from now on. Until I could get away from here.

I sat on the bed in the dark. I was glad I'd answered FB back, but scared stiff he'd take it out on me mam, or me. Needed to cheer meself up, so I put some dirty Amy thoughts into me head. Was just getting to the good part when me mam walked in.

Me mam's got six different ways of saying me name, there's the 'You've-been-good-Danny', the 'You've-been-bad-Danny', the 'That-was-stupid-Danny', the 'Thanks-very-much-Danny,' the 'I-don't-know-what-you-mean-Danny' and the 'You're-in-big-trouble-Danny'. This was definitely the last one.

'Danny…'

'Aye.'

'…I don't like the way you talk to Callum. I also don't like the way you don't talk to Callum.'

'He threw the Christmas lights in the bin.'

'It's his place, Danny.'

'Thought it was our place.'

Me mam folded her arms, the way she does.

'Danny, you can be a right pain.'

'At least I'm not a coward.'

She stood, watching the twinkly lights down the street.

'Is that what you think I am?'

Couldn't drag the word into the trash. I'd said it. 'Aye, I do.' There was just enough light to see me mam bite her lip. 'What's happened to you? What's happened to the mam who shouted at the tattooed bloke?'

Me mam looked like she'd had enough of arguing. Had enough of everything.

'It'll be better when we're married,' she said softly.

'Will he stop hitting you, then? Not what it said on the website.'

'That website isn't about people like us.'

'Yes, it is. It's exactly like us. We are that family. Why can't you see it, Mam? What's the matter with you?'

'I love him, Danny.'

The word gave me the shivers.

'But he doesn't love you.'

Me mam said nothing.

'I will never accept that fat bastard as long as I live. I hate him. I wish he was dead.'

She sat next to me on the bed.

'He says at Easter we can all go to Tenerife. What do you think of that?'

'Just some other hot place he can strangle you.'

Me mam got up from the bed.

'What am I going to do with you?'

She left me room and closed the door.

After what I'd said I waited for it all to kick off downstairs. But instead of shouting, I heard the front door slam. He was off to the pub. Me mam was safe. For a couple of hours.

Don't know how I got to sleep that night, but I did.

Didn't sleep for long.

Me bedroom door burst open, and me mam dashed in, turned the light on and shook me awake. I squinted

at her. Her face looked like she'd seen a monster. FB
must have hit her for what I'd said.

'Mam?'

'It's Callum, he's been attacked.'

Thirty-Eight

•

Attacked? Didn't seem possible. Whickham's not that sort of place.

Got dressed, but me mam got dressed even quicker. She didn't bother with a coat, even though it was freezing outside.

'Come on, Danny,' she shouted, like the house was on fire.

I ran downstairs.

'Where we going?'

'The hospital, where do you bloody think?'

Mam jumped in FB's Range Rover and we headed off. I'd never seen her drive FB's car before. He was

236

the driver in the house. Wouldn't let her near it. Now I knew why. Too fast into the corners, too fast out of the corners, making the engine scream, ignoring all the road signs and signals, generally a nightmare on four wheels.

'What happened?' I said, gripping the seat.

'No idea. Got a call from the police to say he's been attacked.'

'Where?'

'On the way back from the pub.'

Gateshead's definitely gannin to the dogs.

'Who did it?'

'I don't bloody know.'

When me mam swears it means shut your gob.

Didn't take long to get to the hospital, not at that speed. Tyres squealed all the way into the car park. Mam found a spot, but didn't bother to park straight, just switched the engine off, climbed out, and dashed off, without even paying.

I've never seen me mam run so fast, in fact I've never seen me mam run. I sprinted after her, caught up, and we went through some big doors into the hospital. It was dead busy, a man with blood down his face singing at the top of his voice, a woman in her pyjamas holding a baby, both screaming, two girls in short skirts, wrestling on the floor. It was totally mad. More like a mental hospital.

Mam ran over to a desk.

'I'm here to see Callum Jeffries.'

The woman looked at her screen and then a young nurse in a blue dress came over.

'Follow me'.

The nurse walked that fast I had to jog to keep up. After going for miles down the long corridors I spotted a room with two coppers outside.

'Wait here,' said the nurse.

The nurse went into the room while me mam fiddled with her hair. The coppers looked at us as if we were guilty of something. Coppers are trained to have faces like that. Then the nurse came out.

'I'm afraid you can't see him, Miss Croft. He's gone to theatre.'

'Theatre?'

'Yes,' said the nurse. 'For surgery.'

I didn't think me mam's face could get any whiter, but it did. She slumped in a little plastic chair, put there for people about to slump, and held her face in her hands. Then she looked at the two coppers. Maybe they'd have an answer.

'What happened?' she said, looking up at them.

The older copper spoke. He looked like he was the boss. 'We just know that there was some sort of altercation in the street with another man.'

'Mam, what's an altercation?'

'A punch-up.' Mam stared at the copper, her face starving for answers. 'Who with?'

'We're not sure. All we know is that the man who attacked him had a Scottish accent.'

Thirty-Nine

•

Knew what had happened. Me belly told me.

He'd done it.

Me dad had battered FB.

I slumped down on one of the plastic chairs next to me mam. I felt sick. Then I was sick. A nurse came over with a bucket for me and a mop for the floor.

'You okay, Danny?' said me mam, patting me leg.

No, a long, long way from okay. Me dad had come down from Scotland and put me mam's boyfriend in hospital. He'd finally done what I wanted, even though he said he'd never do it in a million years. Think it was the shock that had brought up me tea.

A nurse brought a damp cloth and me mam wiped me brow with it. For once the cold felt good.

'Your colour's come back,' she said.

'Yeah, he's looking more human now,' said the younger copper.

Mam patted me hand. 'I know, Danny, it's been a real shock.'

Aye, but she only knew the half of it.

'I need to speak to the doctors. Will you be okay?'

Nodded.

She went off down the corridor to find out what had happened to FB, while I just sat there, thinking. Was it me dad? Had to be. I mean, what's the chance of a Scotsman battering FB just after I'd asked a Scotsman to batter him? But then I had different thoughts. How did he know where to find Callum? Gateshead's a big place. Had I told him where FB lived? Don't think so. Maybe I did. How did he know which pub to find him at? And how did he know he'd go to the pub tonight?

Maybe it wasn't me dad. But this thought didn't last long. It had to be him. Did more wondering. I wondered what he'd used to attack FB – a knife, a baseball bat, a fist? Probably not a fist, me dad's hands are soft as clarts, and he can only do fifteen press-ups. He wouldn't last long in a fight with a great fat bloke like FB. He must have used something else, maybe a sword, like a Japanese fighter, or an umbrella with a poison tip, like a spy, or maybe a bread knife. Yes, he works in a sandwich shop, definitely a bread knife.

Then I got on to some bad wondering.

I wondered if they could blame me. What if someone figured out I'd been to Scotland, or if they'd heard what I'd asked me dad to do? But the answer to the wonders was: no. Nobody knew I'd been to Scotland, not even Aunty Tina. I hadn't told Barry or Carl or Amy or anyone. And no one had been there when I'd asked me dad to kill him, not Megan, not the neighbours, not Uncle Connor, nobody. Not a single person in the world knew, except me and me dad.

I was starting to hate the hospital now. Even though they'd cleaned the floor, I still got a whiff of pizza-flavoured puke. Then there were all the drunks, like a place full of FBs, the patients with saggy faces and saggy bodies, covered in bandages, and the coppers looking at me, with those copper eyes, trying to see inside me head. I'd had enough of this place. I wanted me bed.

Waited ages.

Me mam finally came back. Saw her right down the corridor, head hanging like it was falling off her body.

'Howway, Danny, let's gan hyem,' she said. I hadn't heard her talk like that in ages, like she didn't care about her words no more.

We walked back down the long corridors, me mam holding me hand, like I was five. We finally got to the front of the hospital and the doors *swooshed* open. Good to be outside, even though it was freezing and raining.

Me mam let go of me hand and we walked across the car park. She stopped and leaned against a ticket machine. I looked at her face. Wet. Couldn't tell whether it was tears or rain.

'Is he okay?'

She shook her head and carried on walking.

The car had got a ticket. Me mam would normally be hacked off about that, but not today. She couldn't be bothered. Just got in and drove off, dead slow, eyes glazed, like someone in a zombie film.

'What happened?' I asked, dying to know.

Mam spoke slow with gaps between her words, like she was speaking to a foreigner.

'Someone had a fight with Callum. He hit his head on the pavement.'

So me dad didn't use a weapon, just used his hands, his soft as bread hands.

Don't know how he managed to knock FB over with those, but he had.

'He's in a bad way, Danny,' said me mam, choking on her words. 'Callum's in a coma.'

Heard of that. It's where you're asleep and find it really hard to wake up. It can go on for ages.

'Will he wake up?'

'God, I hope so.'

I hoped not.

Knew I shouldn't think like that, but I couldn't stop meself. I mean, this was the man who kept hurting me mam. Even if he got better, he'd know what it was like to be well and truly battered. Might make him stop.

Me mam started sobbing. It got so bad she had to stop the car. She couldn't see. We just sat there, on the bypass, engine running, Mam crying.

I couldn't think what she had to cry about. The bloke that punched her, choked her, slapped her, couldn't hurt her. Not tonight any road. Did she feel bad for him, or bad for her? Not the time to ask.

I wanted to give her a hug, but it's hard with your seat belt on, so I gave her arm a little squeeze instead.

'Thanks, Danny, you're a good lad.'

Forty

●

Could hardly sleep a wink for thinking about the coma. What happened when FB came out of it? He might remember who attacked him.

They'd get one of those artists to do a little drawing. Someone might spot that it's Stevie. Then everyone would ask – why would Danny's dad want to come all the way down to Gateshead and punch Danny's mam's boyfriend? Then Aunty Tina would tell me mam about the note. And that would be the end of that.

Must have slept a bit, no idea when. I pulled some tracksuit pants on and a T-shirt and went downstairs. Mam was already at the breakfast table, dressed. She had a cup of smelly tea in front of her. Felt too sick for cereal, so I had a glass of water.

'How ya deein, Mam?'

Ignored me. As usual.

'Why would someone do that to him? And a Scotsman.'

That word made me want to puke again. Funny how one word can do that, first 'Dad', then 'wee', then 'Callum', now 'Scotsman'. Felt me face cherry up, but I don't think Mam noticed. She was too busy staring.

Mam took a tiny sip of her tea, like it was poison.

'Not too many Scotsmen in Gateshead,' she said. 'Shouldn't be too hard to find him.'

What she didn't know was that the Scotsman who did it was now probably miles away in his wee flat.

Then me mam stared at me with a look like she knew something. It made me jump inside.

'Danny, you said that there was a Scots boy at school.'

'Did I?'

'Yes, when you were on the school trip, remember? You told me on the phone.'

'Nowt to do with him.'

'Why not?'

Because the Scots boy doesn't exist.

'Er, just divvent think it will, that's all.'

'But his dad will be Scottish. He must live round here. We'd better tell the police. They'll want to know.'

Me mam got her phone out. She was going to get the coppers round, and get me to tell them about the Scots boy who wasn't there and his invisible dad. Felt all woozy in the head. Mam started tapping her phone. I watched her fingers press the buttons, but they did more than three, a lot more than three. She wasn't calling the police.

'Hello, Louise, it's Kim here,' she said. 'I'm afraid I've got some very bad news for you. It's about Callum.'

Me mam was calling FB's family.

I just sat there, like one of those statue people, listening to her.

'Gone to the pub... call from the police... last night... hit his head... attacked... in a coma.'

She spent the next hour phoning all sorts of people. I had to go to me room. Couldn't stand listening to it, the same story over and over and over.

I rang Amy to tell her what had happened. Even though she now knew what FB was like she said she'd say a Hail Mary for him.

When me mam had finished phoning we went back to the hospital. It wasn't as mad busy as last night, but still mad, with sick people all over the shop. We sat in the waiting room, next to a smelly gadgie with yellow fingers. Forgot me phone, so I had to look through the magazines on the table. They were that old some of the people in it weren't even on the telly no more.

While I was waiting I had a thought. I decided not to call him FB any more, not after what had happened. It didn't seem right. From now on he could have his proper name back. From now on he could be Callum again.

Then a nurse said me mam could go and see him.

'Come on,' she said.

'Me?'

'Please.'

I didn't want to see him. Not now.

Get a grip, Danny.

Got off me chair and went with me mam down the corridors. We reached a room and went in. Thought we'd got the wrong place. Didn't look like a bit like Callum. Just a bloke, his face all puffed up, bandages round his head, eyes closed, tubes everywhere. But the closer you got you could tell it was him. Just.

Me mam went and sat in a chair next to his bed.

'Can he hear us?' said me mam.

'No,' went the nurse.

I stood at the back of the room. Didn't want to look at him.

'Sit next to me, Danny.'

Didn't want to argue. I pulled a chair next to her.

Hated being in the room.

'Can we go now, Mam?'

Ignored me. Again.

I'd' loved to have been able to look inside me mam's

head and see what she was thinking. *I still love him, in spite of everything? Now he knows what it feels like? I won't get hit this week? Bang goes our holiday to Tenerife?*

But her face was giving nothing away.

After what seemed like for ever, she gave me hand a squeeze and we got up.

'See you later, Callum,' she said. 'Love you.'

I said nowt.

We waited at the hospital for Callum's lot to turn up. Recognised some of them from Callum's birthday party, his brother, Ian, his sister, Louise, and his knackered-looking mam. I suppose even blokes that hit mams have mams. But this time they weren't drinking or dancing or laughing. Me dad had seen to that.

'Are you okay, Kim?' said Louise.

Me mam just did a little head move like a pigeon.

'And how's Danny coping?' Like I wasn't even there.

'He's fine.'

Ian gave me mam a hug.

'Shocking,' he said.

No, what was shocking was beating up me mam for no reason at all.

A few of them said hello to me. I tried hard not to look guilty. Don't think anyone spotted that I was. They were too busy being sad.

They soon got round to talking about the attack.

'Just been for a quiet drink,' said Callum's mam.

'Callum quite liked a drink,' said Louise.

No, he *loved* a drink. Couldn't get enough of it.

'Hit by a Scotsman apparently,' said Ian. 'What the flipping heck's a Scotsman doing round here?'

Lisa joined in. 'Police said someone heard them arguing. Callum's not the argumentative type.'

Talking clap-trap. He'd argue with a lamp post when he was drunk.

'Scotsmen are known for their arguing,' said Callum's mam. 'It's in their DNA.'

'Danny knows a Scots boy at school, don't you, Danny?' said me mam.

All the eyes in the waiting room suddenly turned on me, even the smelly gadgie. It felt like class, when you've been found out.

'A Scots boy, you say?' went Ian, eyes narrowing. 'You'd better go tell that policeman,' he said, looking at a copper standing by a wall covered in posters about diseases.

I looked at the copper, the copper looked at me. I was going to have to speak to him. Everyone was watching, waiting. I put me magazine down, got up from the chair and walked towards the copper dead slow, like a death march. What was I going to say? If I told him there was a Scots boy in our school, he'd ask, 'Who is he?' Then he'd ask, 'Who's his dad?' And I'd just stand there like a bus stop.

Was right next to the copper now. I could feel every-one watching, their eyes drilling holes into me brain.

'Hello,' he said, smiling, as he looked down. He was even taller than Lanky Dave. He had a friendly face, though, for a copper.

'Hello,' I went.

They were all waiting for me to tell him. Luckily, they weren't close enough to hear what I said.

'Do you know where the toilets are?'

'Yes, they're just down the corridor, on the left.' Hadn't said enough yet. They were still watching. 'How do you become a copper?'

He laughed a bit. Hope they didn't spot that. They'd think, 'Why's a copper laughing about the hunt for a dangerous Scotsman?'

'Well, you've got to grow a bit first,' said the copper. 'Then you've got to go to college, pass some exams, go on the beat.'

'Ta.'

'Oh, and by the way, we're called police officers, not coppers.'

'Sorry.'

I walked slowly back.

Me mam put her arm around me. 'Well done, Danny.'

Forty-One

• •

That night two coppers came round, one bloke copper, one woman copper. Mam and Louise sat on the sofa. I sat on a chair in the corner, the coppers sat on two chairs from the kitchen. It was like having a cop programme in our own front room.

'Can you tell us about what happened last night, Kim?' said the woman copper, with her notebook out.

Yeah, tell them about him tearing the Christmas lights down.

Me mam looked at the floor. 'Not really,' she said. 'Callum left about eight o'clock I think. He went to The Flying Fox, as normal.'

'So Callum went to the pub a lot?' Bloke copper picked up on that. Can be quite clever coppers.

'He was trying to cut back, but, yes, he went a bit.'

'How often?' said the woman copper.

'Four times a week, I guess, sometimes five.'

Aye, and then he bashes me mam. She should have told them that, perfect opportunity, got two coppers in your front room. You don't get that every day. But me mam didn't say it. Maybe she felt bad that Callum was now the one all bashed up, or maybe she didn't want to say it in front of his sister.

'Did he go to any other pubs?' Woman copper.

'Don't think so. The Flying Fox is only ten minutes' walk away. Callum didn't like walking much.'

'Did he have any enemies?' Bloke copper.

Me.

'Did he have any enemies?' repeated me mam. She looked in my direction when she said this, making me guts squash up inside. Then she looked away. 'Don't think so.'

'Did he have friends at the pub?' Bloke copper.

'If he did he never talked about them. He used to take his tablet, or his F1 magazine. I think he just kept himself to himself.'

I'd seen him through the pub window on his own. Me mam was right about that one.

'How long have you lived with him?' Woman copper.

'We've been in this house since last December, isn't that right, Danny?'

'Aye.'

One year too long.

'Have you spoken to the people in the pub?' said me mam. Now she'd turned into a copper.

The woman copper nodded. 'Yes, we're taking statements from everyone who was there.'

Silly question, Mam. 'Course they take statements. That's the number one part of their job.

'Has Callum ever got into trouble with anyone?' Bloke copper.

I crossed me fingers tight. Come on, Mam, now's your chance. Tell them, tell them what he did, tell him he got into trouble – with you.

'No.'

I looked at her. But she wouldn't look at me.

Why didn't she tell them about the fights? Why didn't she tell them about the lass on the coast road? Why didn't she tell them what an evil bastard he was? I wished with all me brain for me mam to say it, but she didn't, just silence, like nothing had ever happened in our house.

I wanted to tell them what really went on, but if I did they'd turn their eyes on me, and they'd want to know why I was so angry and why I hated Callum so much.

Then they'd find out everything.

The woman copper spotted a *Brides* magazine. 'You and Callum were going to get married?'

'Are,' said me mam.

'Sorry,' said the woman copper.

It wasn't much of a mistake but it was enough to start me mam crying. Louise shuffled over and put an arm around her.

'It's all right, Kim,' said Louise.

Me mam stopped after a bit. It wasn't one of her massive cries.

The coppers started again.

'Did you have a previous boyfriend?' Woman copper.

Mam looked a bit shifty.

'Not for a long time.' Me mam looked at me, like she was guilty of something. 'I had a couple of short relationships.'

Must have been dead short. Don't even remember them.

The woman copper glanced at me. 'And what about Danny's father?'

Wazzocks.

Mam looked down at her nails, like the memory was messing with her head. 'We're not in touch. I haven't seen him for years, since before Danny was born.'

Please don't say it, please don't say it, please don't say it, please don't say he lives in Scotland, please don't say it. I held me breath that long I thought I was going to pass out, but me mam didn't breathe a word. The God of Please Don't Say It had heard me.

Louise scratched the fish on her leg. 'Have you got any clues?'

The bloke copper answered. 'All we've got to go on is what we heard from a woman in Amberly Close. She was putting her rubbish out and heard a man with a Scottish accent shouting abuse. When she went to take a look Callum was lying on the ground, but the Scotsman had gone.'

The woman copper looked at Mam. 'Have you any idea why anyone would hold a grudge against him?'

Me mam didn't look at me. She just shrugged. 'He works in IT, likes watching motor racing, he's not in any trouble. He's not a drug dealer or anything.'

'Did Callum have any dealings up in Scotland?'

'He used to travel a bit on business, but it was down south – Birmingham, Reading, London, places like that. I don't think he's ever been to Scotland. I never heard him mention it.'

Silence.

The coppers had run out of questions. Typical. I could have thought of loads more. They grabbed their hats and stood up. Before they left the bloke copper had one more thing to say, just like they do on telly.

'I know it's a very difficult time for you, Kim, but

if anything comes to you, anything at all, please don't hesitate to call.'

Mam nodded.

The woman copper put a hand on Mam's shoulder. 'I'm sure everything will be okay.'

Mam gave a small smile.

'Yeah, Callum will be fine,' she said. 'He's as strong as an ox.'

Forty-Two

•

On the eleventh of December, Callum Jeffries died.

The punch had done its business. You'd have thought with all the NHS money and all those doctors and nurses and machines and drugs and stuff they'd be able to do something. It was only a punch, not a missile. But they couldn't save him, he just went and died.

I'll never forget the morning me mam got the call. I was brushing me teeth when I heard a scream like you've never heard in your life, worse than a horror film. I dropped me toothbrush, ran downstairs, and found Louise on the kitchen floor, screaming. She'd been staying with us since he got hit. Me mam was on the floor next to her, holding her.

'Nooooo,' went Louise.

Didn't need to ask what had happened.

Normally make me mam a cup of tea when she's upset, but a cup of tea was never going to sort this out. Was weird seeing two grown-ups clinging to each other, lying on the floor like that. I didn't want to watch them, so I went and sat on a chair in the front room. Realised I was sitting where he sat. Could feel the giant hollow his bum had made. I felt sick again, like when he was screaming at me mam, and on the train back from Edinburgh, and the night at the hospital, and all the other times.

Me mind was mushed up. What I'd dreamed about for months and months had finally happened. So why was I feeling so weird? Me mam was finally going to be okay. She wasn't going to be one of the two women. I'd done it. I'd made it happen. Can you be blamed for doing something good?

I looked around and saw the F1 magazines he'd never read again, the massive telly he'd never watch again, the coasters he'd never put his drinks on again. And outside, the Range Rover he'd never break the law in again.

I felt a tear pop into me eyeball.

What the heck was that doing there?

Maybe it was just the shock of the news or the sound of sobbing. I went out into the garden to get away from the noise. I didn't care that it was freezing outside, I needed some air, any air would do. Felt like me head had been put in a blender.

Went round the back of the shed like I did when Callum was screaming at me mam after Christmas dinner. After a bit she came out in her dressing gown. She didn't care about the cold either, just sat on the frosty grass and wrapped her arms around me. Didn't look like me mam any more, her eyes red, her face a weird colour, her hair all over the shop where Louise had been cuddling her.

'He's gone, Danny.'

I felt her tears landing on top of me head, soft and warm. One trickled down me face, like it belonged to me. I felt bad. I'd done this to her. If I'd gone on the school trip to the Lakes none of this would have happened. Callum would be off to work, Mam would be down the call centre, and I'd be off to school. Everything would be normal. This was as un-normal as you could get.

We stayed like this for ages. Was starting to get a cramp in me leg. But I couldn't shift me mam. Just had to swallow the pain.

Finally, she got up.

'Let's go inside,' she said. 'It's freezing out here.'

Louise must have phoned the others because they all started showing up, Ian, his mam, and the ones whose names I'd forgotten. Then our lot turned up, Gran and

Granda, Aunty Tina and Uncle Greg, Uncle Martin and Aunty Sheila, and a couple of me mam's mates I hadn't seen since before he turned up. Everyone ended up in the kitchen, talking in whispers.

School hadn't broken up yet, but me mam made me stay at home. It was the first time in me life I'd ever wanted to go to school.

'Why can't I gan?'

''Cos I need you here, Danny.'

I don't know what she needed me for. Hadn't I done enough already? I left a message on Amy's phone. Told her what had happened and asked her to come and see me after school.

Couldn't stay in the kitchen all day, it was too dangerous. They might ask a question, like, 'What's the news on the Scots boy at school?' Or, 'How was your school trip?' And to make it worse Aunty Tina was there. The one who knew I knew where me dad lived.

Went up to me room and lay on me bed. The day dragged like a tortoise's belly. Me mam didn't make me lunch or tea, but for once I couldn't care less. Wasn't hungry.

Round about six the front door bell went. It was Amy. She came up to me room and we lay on me bed, staring at the ceiling, holding hands. I knew me mam wouldn't come in. Not today.

'How's your mam?'

'Upset.'

'In spite of…'

'Aye, in spite of…'

'And how are you?'

'A bit weird.'

'You're glad he's gone, though, aren't you?'

'Aye.'

'You don't sound glad.'

Because you don't know the half of it, Amy.

'Just the shock. That's all.'

Amy leaned over and kissed me on the cheek. 'You'll get over it, Danny.'

Maybe.

'Told me mam and dad. They said that if there's anything they can do to help.'

'Aye, they could invent a time machine and make me mam go back and meet a man who loves her, and looks after her, and never, ever hurts her.'

'You are so sweet, Danny Croft.' Then she kissed me once more and jumped off the bed. 'I've gotta run. I'm going to Confession tonight. I'll see you at school.'

Was glad when bed time finally turned up, but when it did I wished it hadn't.

Couldn't sleep. Me head still spinning round and round, Scotland, Stevie, Callum, the punch, me, Scotland, Stevie, Callum, the punch, me.

Next morning I heard the letterbox go. Went

downstairs and got *The Journal* off the mat. The head-line nearly made me heave.

ATTACK VICTIM DIES

I kept staring at it, like it wasn't real. But it was. I could feel it with me fingers. I took the paper into Callum's office and sat down at the desk to read. It said that the police had launched a murder inquiry. That was the bit in big black letters. The story underneath was the one I already knew. Callum Jeffries, thirty-eight, was attacked on his way home from The Flying Fox pub in Whickham last Friday night. It didn't mention the punch or the Scotsman. It said he was taken for emergency surgery, but he died as a result of his injury.

There was a picture of Callum, smiling, as usual. Mam or one of his lot must have given it to them. I'd never seen it before. Made him look like a normal bloke, not one with spit on his lips and angry fists. People would look at it and say, 'He looks canny, who could do such a thing?'

Put the paper in the recycling when I'd finished. I didn't want me mam seeing it. It would only set her off again.

The coppers came back to speak to me mam. They were dead serious this time. Me mam didn't have much to say, but the coppers did. Kept asking questions. Probably the only murder they had.

'I've told you all I know,' said me mam, getting fed up. 'Why not speak to the people in the pub? Someone must have seen something.'

'We're looking into that,' said the woman copper.

Hoped so. But you never know with coppers. They always make mistakes on the telly. Probably made loads already.

Then me mam had a question for them.

'Have you found the Scotsman yet?'

'We're speaking to various Scottish men in the area,' said the bloke copper, as though Mam had asked a really stupid question.

I was scared that any second me mam would say, 'Have you spoken to the Scots boy at school yet, the one that Danny knows?'

But the question never came. It lay buried. And the coppers picked up their hats and went off to look for Scotsmen.

Mam sat on the sofa, lank hair hanging down over her white face.

'Do you want a cup of tea, Mam?'

She nodded.

When I came back she was crying again. I put the tea on the table and saw what she was crying about, a magazine lying on the floor, just one word on the front. *Brides*.

Forty-Three

• • •

They cremated Callum on the nineteenth of December.

Before we left Gateshead for the cremation I burned the note from Aunty Tina. It was too dangerous. I also washed the ball me dad gave me in case his fingerprints were on it. I even wiped me sports bag in case he'd touched it. I didn't want anything that could lead them back to him.

I'd asked if Amy could come, but her mam and dad wouldn't let her. We went off in Aunty Tina's car. I wished I could have gone in the other car with Uncle

Martin, Aunty Sheila and Gran and Granda. Every time I looked at her I thought of the note, but Aunty Tina never said a thing. She looked at me funny a couple of times. I think she knew she shouldn't have done it, but she kept her secret wrapped up in her head, and I kept mine.

I'd never been to a funeral before. Me mam borrowed a black suit from a friend. Everyone wore black that day, black suits, black shoes, black dresses, black ties, black hats, black everything. It went with the weather. Black clouds, wherever you looked.

There weren't many kids at the funeral. I only counted five. No idea who they were. Aunty Tina had left her two behind with Uncle Greg. Said they were too young. Grown-ups try and keep bairns away from stuff like that. Not sure why. They leave the news on, with people being killed, blown up, heads chopped off, massacred. But I suppose it's different when it's somewhere else. This was here.

Callum got cremated in a little room next to a grave-yard. We sat in the very front row. I normally like being at the front, like on a roller coaster, or the top deck of a bus, but for once I wished I'd been at the back. Didn't want to see what was going on. Some of Callum's lot got up and said canny things about him, like how clever he was, and what a good driver he was, and how he loved his family and nephews and nieces and stuff like that.

They also mentioned me mam.

'Callum loved Kim,' said Louise, pausing to blow her nose. 'He knew he'd found a real diamond when he found her. She made him happy. And I hope she found happiness with him.'

Nearly laughed.

'He was such a kind, thoughtful man.'

Me mam squeezed me hand tight. We knew different.

Not one of them said anything bad about him. Guess you're not allowed to slag people off at their funerals. When they'd finished talking, the curtains in front of the coffin closed, like at the cinema, and that was it. The end. We trudged out as some American gadgie sang a song called 'My Way'. I wondered if me mam had chosen it, 'cos the last words were about taking the blows. I'd ask her some time. Not today.

After the funeral, we all went to Callum's brother's house. It was even bigger than ours. It had three garages, a garden that looked like a park, six toilets, and a telly the size of a ping-pong table. They put cartoons on for the kids. I don't normally watch them, but did today. Was better than standing round waiting for a question. Everyone else just stood in the kitchen with cups of tea, eating little sandwiches, speaking with the volume down, like they were in class.

I wanted to go in the garden and play football, but Mam said I couldn't. Not when someone's died. I wondered how long you had to wait after a funeral to play football. Before a match they just have a minute's silence when someone's dead, then start. That's a much better idea. Don't know why we couldn't do that.

After tea and sandwiches me mam said goodbye to everybody. There was lots more kissing and hugging and crying. A few of them hugged me. Then we got in Aunty Tina's car and drove back to Gateshead. There's nothing in the world more boring than a motorway, especially when the traffic's bad, your mam's sad, no one's talking, and you've done something you shouldn't. But that's what it was like, all the way back.

Aunty Tina dropped us home. Me mam and her sister hugged for ages.

'Be strong, Kim.'

'I'll try,' said me mam.

'And you look after her,' said Aunty Tina, looking at me.

It was weird going back into the house of a dead man. Every time I turned a corner I expected to see him, smiling, rubbing me hair, giving me money, calling me General. But if ever I found myself feeling a bit sad for him, I reminded myself of one thing – he would never ever hurt me mam again.

Christmas came, but it didn't feel like it. We didn't have a tree, not even a plastic one. It just felt like a normal day with presents. We could have put up the lights Callum didn't want, but don't think me mam could be bothered. Got her some skin lotion stuff and a tin with loads of different chocolate biscuits. She'd not have to worry about eating them again. Mam got me a games console and a Newcastle United away kit. Really liked it, but felt guilty about smiling too much.

'Merry Christmas, Danny,' she said.

'Merry Christmas, Mam.'

It didn't seem right to be saying merry anything when your mam's bloke's been killed, but you've got to say it at Christmas. It's just one of those things.

Went to see Amy.

I gave her some more perfume. She got me a T-shirt. Gave her a kiss and a hug. But it wasn't like last Christmas. A bad feeling in the air. I wanted to spend the day with her, but me mam said I couldn't. We went to Aunty Tina's instead. I still felt funny every time I saw her, thinking she'd say something. *'Did you write to your dad, Danny? Did you send him a Christmas card?'* But she never said a word, and I got the feeling she never would.

There was a massive meal with roast turkey and stuffing and stuff, but I didn't eat much. I noticed me mam wasn't eating either, just pushing the food about on her plate like she didn't know what to do with it. There was a big shortage of laughing this year. At least there'd be no argument about driving home. Aunty Tina had got us a taxi.

I thought about me dad, and wondered what he was doing now. Probably having turkey in his flat, watching films on telly. I wondered if Megan was back from Cowdenbeath. I also couldn't stop thinking about *it*. I hadn't hit Callum, but I might as well have done. I'd made the punch happen, I'd put the death idea in me dad's head. He'd never have done it if I hadn't asked him. I mean, you don't drive a hundred and four miles in the dark to go and lamp someone you don't know for nothing, do you?

I started to think, hope, that me dad hadn't done it. I mean, he said he wouldn't do it, didn't he? He'd said it loads of times, said it was for someone else to sort out. Maybe me dad had paid another Scotsman to do it, or maybe Callum met a Scots bloke in the street and said something bad to him. Could imagine him doing that. The Scots bloke would then punch him to show that he didn't like what he'd said. Callum would fall and hit his head. That's what could have happened.

Though it probably didn't.

Ever since the attack I couldn't sleep properly. Luckily, it was now the Christmas holidays and I could lie in bed for ages or just crash on the sofa. Me mam couldn't find the energy to nag me. But when school started, the teachers couldn't wait to start nagging.

'Wakey, wakey, Danny,' said Mr Hetherington. 'Bears hibernate in winter, not humans.'

Laugh, laugh, laugh.

'Croft, stop yawning,' shouted Mr Tobin in PE. 'I can see what you've had for breakfast and it's making me ill.'

Laugh, laugh, laugh.

Even Amy was on me case.

'Danny, I don't get it. I thought you'd be happy. Your mam's safe now.'

'I am happy about that.'

'So what aren't you happy about?'

Shrugged. Too tired to lie.

Amy looked deep into me eyes, like an optician.

'I'd love to know what's going on in that head of yours.'

Forty-Four

•

In the middle of all this, something good actually happened. Lanky Dave got expelled. One minute he was at school, the next he wasn't.

Amy had gone to see the teachers.

'Seeing as it's the start of a new year, I decided it was time for a change,' she said. 'I did what you asked, Danny. I told them all about Dave.'

Gobsmacked.

'You were right. It was never going to get any better. I was just being pathetic.'

I honestly thought Amy would be just like me mam, and let it go on and on and on.

First time anyone had ever listened to what I'd said. Make that the second.

'I told Mr Hetherington, and he took me to see Mrs Brighton. They got Lanky Dave. He lied, of course, and said he'd done nothing. But when they checked his phone they found everything. Guilty on all counts.'

Was dead proud of Amy, and bought her a massive hot chocolate with cream. But three days after the good news, came the bad news.

Funny thing about really bad stuff – you just don't see it coming, like the ball that hits you in the face or that impossible question in class that your brain's not ready for. It was like that with my bad thing. I think everyone in the world gets one day like that. This was mine.

I'd been with Amy at the park after school. We were chilling out on the roundabout, just holding hands, talking, laughing. I gave her a kiss goodnight, as always, got on me bike and cycled home up Whickham Bank. But whichever way I went the wind seemed to be blowing into me, like it was trying to stop me getting back. I only thought this afterwards.

As soon as I turned into our street, I saw it, a car, outside our house. The car looked like one I'd seen before. Couldn't figure out where. Me heart started hammering away. Don't know why, it was only a car, but something told me it meant news, bad news.

I wheeled me bike round the side of the house and

went in the kitchen, still asking me brain the same question – who does that car belong to? But me brain was being stupid as usual. Maybe it was too full of Amy. I could hear voices from the front room. It was me mam and a bloke. The other voice sounded like one I'd heard before, but it wasn't clear enough. Too much door in the way.

I walked towards the front room. The voices got louder, but the extra volume didn't help, I still couldn't figure out who the second voice belonged to. I put me sweaty hand on the handle, counted to ten, and opened the door.

Mr Hetherington turned to look at me.

'Hello, Danny,' he said.

'Hello, sir,' I said back.

Me mam was sitting next to him. I could tell from their faces they weren't just having a nice chat. It was serious.

'What's going on?' I said.

'Nothing to worry about, Danny,' said Mr Hetherington. 'I just wanted to talk to your mum about your behaviour at school.'

Behaviour? What did he mean by that? It couldn't be about Lanky Dave on the stairs, that was ages ago. Any road, he'd been expelled. I hadn't been answering back at the teachers and me and Amy were careful not to touch in school.

'What sort of behaviour, Mr Hetherington?' I said, in me poshest voice.

'You just seem tired all the time, Danny.'

Is that all?

'Aye, get a bit sleepy sometimes.'

'It's more than sometimes, Danny,' said Mr Hetherington. 'I've spoken to the other teachers, it's nearly every day.'

'Sit down, Danny,' said me mam.

Did as me mam said and sat on a chair next to them. They were both holding cups, me mam's best ones. Noticed me mam's cup was shaking, as though she'd been at the sauce.

'I know you've been going through a difficult time, Danny, but you'd tell us if there was something troubling you?'

'Of course, sir.'

The mountain of lies just kept getting bigger and bigger.

'Falling asleep in lessons isn't normal, Danny,' said Mr Hetherington.

'Danny always used to be a good sleeper.'

That was before everything.

'What time does he go to bed?' asked Mr Hetherington.

'About ten.'

'Maybe it's worth having a word with the doctor,' said Mr Hetherington.

And then she looked at him and said the words that would change everything. 'I bet he wasn't like this on the school trip?'

I swear me heart nearly stopped. The trip was long gone, it had become history, like the Romans. But now here it was, in me front room, dug up, alive, and me mam and me teacher were going to ask me questions about it. Never felt so petrified in me whole life.

Mr Hetherington looked baffled. 'School trip? But Danny didn't go on the school trip.'

As his words took hold the mouths of me mam and Mr Hetherington flopped open like goldfish.

I knew there and then that it was all over. They'd want to know what had happened. They'd want to know where I'd gone, what I'd done, who I'd seen. I wanted to die. But me heart had other ideas. Sending blood around and around me as fast as it could.

Me mam glared at me with a face she could have borrowed off Callum.

'You didn't go on the school trip?' she said, her voice growing louder with every word.

I wanted to lie. I wanted to lie so much, and say that I did go, but how could I do that? Mr Hetherington had been on it, so had the other teachers. Nobody saw me. I was the ghost of the school trip.

Could feel tears stabbing at me eyes. 'No, Mam, I didn't go.'

She got up and stood right in front of me.

'Well, if you didn't go on the school trip, where the hell did you go?'

Forty-Five

• •

Told them. Had to.

It might have been different if Mr Hetherington hadn't been there. I might have made something up, something me mam might believe, something that could dig me out of the massive hole I was now in. But I knew there was no way out.

'Scotland.'

'Scotland?' said me mam. Her face couldn't have looked more surprised if I'd said 'the moon'.

Nodded.

'What in God's name were you doing up in Scotland?'

Mr Hetherington had heard enough. I think he

knew there was a gigantic storm coming. One he could never stop.

'I'd better be on my way,' he said, standing up. 'I think this is for you two to sort out.' He put his coat on and picked up his briefcase. 'Thanks for the tea and biscuits, Miss Croft.' But Mam said nothing. She was too busy glaring at me. 'I'll let myself out.'

Wish I could have gone with him.

I heard the front room door close, then the front door, then his car door, then I heard his car start, then I heard him drive off. It was just me mam and me in the house. I never thought I'd be scared of her, but I was scared now.

Kept me eyes glued on the carpet. I could see me mam's feet. She hadn't moved, like she was frozen solid. But her mouth wasn't frozen, and I knew it wouldn't be long before the questions came back, including the one I never wanted to answer.

'Danny, what on earth were you doing up in Scotland?'

Me mam didn't have the nice voice any more, the one she's got for her job, the one that makes people spend money. That voice had packed its bags and gone away. A new voice had moved in, a loud, ugly one.

'Danny, I'm talking to you,' she practically screamed.

I couldn't look at her. Me own mam. Kept staring down. I wanted to disappear too, become invisible like a superhero. That's what I wanted more than anything in the world, not to be here. I wanted to be with Amy, in the garden shed, her arms tight around me. Or in Scotland, in me dad's flat. But I couldn't escape. If I went off on me bike she'd chase me in Callum's car. Even if I rode as fast as anything she'd catch me. And if I went up the alleyway where cars can't go, she'd get her phone out and call the police. They'd send bikes and dogs. They'd find me and bring me back. And Mam would still be there, with the same face on, with the same question – what were you doing up in Scotland?

Why didn't I say 'London'? Could have said I'd gone on an adventure. She might have believed that, but it was too late. The name had escaped. What was I going to tell her? I didn't know anyone in Scotland, at least no one I was meant to know. Could say I went there because I'd never been before, and leave it at that, but Mam would talk to people, she'd talk to her sister. Aunty Tina knew about the address, she'd tell me mam, maybe not today, but one day. They'd find out. Like Megan found out about me. They'd piece it all together. The jigsaw of me great big lie.

I looked up from the carpet. Didn't want to lie no more. I was sick of it. I'm not a bairn. I've got a girlfriend. It was time for the truth.

'I went to see me dad.'

Mam looked at me like I'd turned into the devil.

Then she started screaming, like she'd gone totally mad. I love me mam, I do. But I needed to get away from her. Needed to be anywhere but here. The screams told me everything.

She knew.

I tried to run for the door, but mam caught me by the wrist and threw me hard on the sofa. She was breathing so heavy that she couldn't speak, like when Callum grabbed her in Spain. But when she did find her words her voice came out extra small.

'He killed him, didn't he? Steve killed Callum.'

Head spinning. It felt like the time I swallowed water when Callum pushed me in. Underwater, drowning, not enough air, not enough anything. Struggling. No one to help me.

She grabbed me by the shoulders. 'He's the one who hit him. It's him, isn't it?'

I didn't want to tell her, but I knew there was no point in lying. The truth was too big to hide. Me mam would find out. Mams always find out.

'Aye.'

Mam loosened her grip on me shoulders, then she fell backwards on to the sofa like she'd been shot by a sniper. She just sat there staring at me. I wanted to cry, but even me tears were too scared to come out. I needed to get to Scotland to warn me dad, tell him they'd becoming for him. But there'd be coppers at the station, on the train, there's coppers everywhere. They'd stop me.

Mam's voice finally came back. 'Why?'

I'd said too much already.

Jumped up and ran to the door. But she got there before me, and slammed it shut. I pulled on the handle. No good. All her weight was on it. All the weight Callum had been trying to get rid of.

Mam grabbed me by the collar. 'You're not going anywhere till you've told me,' she said menacingly.

I tried to pull the handle again, but Mam was super strong. I couldn't escape. She scrunched me collar dead tight around me throat.

'Why?' she screamed, right in me face.

''Cos he hit you,' I screamed back.

I could sense me mam's fingers easing off. She let go of me collar. I could feel her breath on me face slowing down. She knew I'd done the right thing. She knew I'd done it for her.

Then me mam hit me.

She'd never done it before, not even when I'd scratched me name on the kitchen chair, or when I smashed a ball through the bathroom window. But she'd done it now. *Bang*. I lay curled up on the floor like dog mess. Me face hurt, but what hurt most was inside. I'd tried to help me mam, I really had, but I'd only ended up hurting her. Now she was hurting me.

Nothing made sense any more.

'What gave you the right to do something like that?' she shouted.

'What gave him the right to hit you?'

Me mam took some little gulps in.

'Yes, he did things maybe he shouldn't, but the reason I put up with it was because of *you*.'

I must be hearing things.

'*Me?*'

'Yes, you, Danny. I wanted you to have all the things I couldn't give you. Stuck in that little flat together. We were never going to get anywhere. You know all those things I bought for your birthday, for Christmas? It was with money given me by your Aunty Tina. I've never had anything, Danny. Nothing. Callum was our way out. Couldn't you see that?'

No, I could not see that.

'You did all that just for a house?'

'Not just a house, Danny. It was everything. The food, the clothes, the holidays, the money. All the stuff I couldn't give you in a million years.'

'Mam, it was just stuff.'

'Yeah, stuff you loved. I remember the look on your face the first time you saw this place.'

'What's the point in having a nice house if you're dead?'

'Callum wasn't going to kill me.'

'Mam, a hundred and four women every year who think they won't end up dead, end up dead.'

'Why didn't you tell me all this, Danny?'

'I did tell you, Mam, over and over, but you wouldn't listen, would you? You'd listen to him, that fat bastard, but not me, never me. Why didn't you tell me you were getting beaten up because of me?'

A great big silence fell on the room, like an invisible boulder crushing us both. We lived in the same house, under the same roof, sat on the same sofa, watched the same telly, saw each other every day, and not once could we find the time to say why we were doing what we were doing. Our silence had come back to punish us.

Me mam slid down the wall and sat on the floor next to me, and put her face in her hands, sobbing.

No words for a long, long time.

'I'm sorry I hit you, Danny.'

'It's okay, Mam.'

It wasn't. But this was one lie I didn't mind telling.

'What did you say to your dad?'

'I asked him to get rid of Callum.'

'What did he say?'

'Na.'

Thought there was still a small chance he hadn't done it.

'It might have been another Scotsman,' I said.

Mam snorted. 'If it's the same Steve I remember, he did it, all right.'

'What are you gonna do?'

'I'm gonna call the police.'

I got down on me knees, me hands grabbing her tracksuit pants, me eyes begging her.

'Please, Mam, don't call them. He didn't mean to kill Callum, he didn't want to do it, he didn't want to do anything, it was all my idea.'

I imagined in me head what would happen. Me dad at home with Megan, watching telly, then the coppers bursting through the door with guns, Megan screaming, me dad being pushed to the carpet, handcuffed, dragged away, all because of me.

'Please.'

'I'm sorry, Danny.'

'Don't call them.'

But nothing I say works on me mam.

She called them.

The coppers were round that quick you'd think we had burglars. They spoke to me mam in the kitchen, then they spoke to me. I didn't want to stitch me dad up, but I'd said way too much already, so I told them everything. It was about time somebody knew what Callum was like, I mean, really like, behind that smile, that stupid pretend smile.

The coppers flew into action.

They went to Scotland, got me dad and brought him back to Tyneside. The one place he never wanted to be.

Forty-Six

•

They took me to the police station with me mam. I didn't want to go there. It's where Callum should have been sent, not me. But me mam just told me to be strong and tell them everything.

Got taken into a room with no wallpaper or pictures or anything. It was just like I'd seen on telly, except this time it was me in the question seat. Apart from the coppers there was another person there too – Mrs Stocksfield, my solicitor. She seemed dead friendly. Told me to just tell the police everything that had happened.

So that's what I did.

Went right back to the time he first turned up.

'I think me mam found FB on the internet.'

'Who's FB?' asked a copper in a suit.

His nickname had slipped out.

'Fat Bastard,' I said.

The coppers had a smile about that.

'Can we call him Callum from now on, Danny?'

'Aye.'

I didn't just make him sound like the devil. Said that he was canny at first, giving me money, rubbing me hair, taking us into his big house. But then I told them about the bad stuff, making fun of me mam, shouting at me mam, and finally, beating me mam.

Then I told them about what I found on the internet. Two women killed every week. Was scared me mam was going to end up like them. Dead. That's when I decided to do something about it. To save me mam, I had to kill him.

'So you found your dad, and you asked him to kill Callum?' asked a copper.

Nodded.

'Nods are no good, Danny. We need a yes or no.'

Forgot they were recording it.

'Aye, I asked me dad to kill FB, sorry, Callum.'

'And what was your dad's reaction?' asked the copper.

'He said, no way, not in a million years.'

'Why did he say that?'

'Said it wasn't his problem. That it was up to me mam to sort out. Said she was nothing to do with him.'

Don't know if the coppers were happy me with answers or not. Their faces were like sheets of blank paper.

'I had a canny time with me dad. But he said he'd never do anything about Callum. Then I came home.'

They finally stopped asking questions and switched their recorder off.

'Well done, Danny,' said Mrs Stocksfield.

They left me in the room with a woman copper, while the others went somewhere else. Mrs Stocksfield came back, and sat in the chair opposite me, a serious look on her face.

'They're going to let you go,' she said. 'But they need to speak to the Crown Prosecution Service.'

'About what?'

'About whether you've committed a crime. Conspiracy to kill is a criminal offence.'

'What's conspiracy?'

'Working together.'

Felt what little food was in me stomach trying to escape. 'Will I go to prison?'

'I can't say, Danny.'

Mam told her story to the coppers, and then she took me home. I was sick out of the taxi window. The thought of going to prison was every bit as bad as living with Callum.

I was told not to go to school. Couldn't even contact Amy. The police had taken me phone and the laptop to look for evidence. Also took me passport to stop me leaving the country. Me mam said it was best if I just stayed in the house.

They were the longest days of me life. Not just worrying about what would happen to me dad, but what would happen to me. The thought of being banged up, away from me mam, Amy, me mates, was as bad as anything that had been in me head this past year.

Me mam asked me how I knew where to find me dad.

Told her me final lie.

Said I met a bloke in the park who knew him, and where he lived.

Think me mam knew I was lying, but didn't have the strength to argue.

Three days later Mrs Stocksfield came to the house with a woman copper. I tried to read their faces for the news, but they were like shop-window dummies.

We all sat in the front room, Mrs Stocksfield, the copper, me mam, me.

'I've got some good news for you, Danny,' said Mrs Stocksfield. 'The police have spoken to the Crown Prosecution Service and they're not going to bring any charges against you.'

'Effing belter.'

'Danny!'

'Sorry, Mam, Mrs Stocksfield, officer.'

'They've spoken to your dad, Danny,' said Mrs Stocksfield. 'His story tallies with yours. The CPS have said that there's no evidence of conspiracy or planning between you two.'

Felt like running round the room punching the air. But the good news didn't last.

'Your dad, however, has been charged with murder.'

'But he promised to see me. We agreed. We're going to meet up when I'm eighteen.'

'You've got to let the courts decide what happens,' said Mrs Stocksfield.

'But murderers get life. He's got his job at the sandwich shop.'

Me mam held me to her chest, just like the day that Callum died.

Mrs Stocksfield and the woman copper left.

I needed to speak to Amy. She came round that night.

'Danny, what's going on?' she said, as she ran into me room. 'Why've you not been at school? I've been texting you like crazy, what's happening? Everyone at school's talking about you. People are saying you've been arrested.'

'I've not been arrested.'

'So what's going on?'

Was terrified of telling Amy, but I knew I had to.

Told her the lot.

When I'd finished, Amy just sat there on me bed, looking at me, like I was someone else. Thought she'd be proud of me.

'Danny, you stupid, stupid idiot.' Felt like I'd been hit again. 'Getting your dad to kill Callum. Why didn't you go to the police?'

Don't know what was worse. Amy calling me an idiot, or knowing that everything I'd done was wrong. She turned away, like she couldn't bear to look at me.

'Amy, you've no idea what it was like living in this house. Everything in your family is so perfect. Imagine your mam's getting beaten, all the time, and won't do a thing to save herself. What would you do?'

'Not this. I'd never do this. You should have told me, Danny, you really should have told me. You're my boyfriend. We're meant to tell each other stuff. You don't solve problems like this by keeping them to yourself.'

'You didn't tell anyone about Lanky Dave.'

'No, not at the start. But I did. I plucked up the courage. You're the one who persuaded me. Why didn't you do the same? Where was your courage, Danny?'

Good question. Where was me courage? I'd found it once, when I pushed Lanky Dave down the stairs. Was that it? My one bit of courage used up. I was too chicken to tell Amy. Too chicken to tell me relatives. Too chicken to tell the police. Just too chicken.

Deep down I knew that Amy was right. I should have talked to her. Somebody. Anybody. Instead I'd talked to the one person who had nothing to do with it, and got him charged with murder. I'd made the world's biggest ever cock-up.

'I'm sorry,' I said.

'I'm sorry too.'

Amy got up off the bed, and looked at me with a face I'd never seen before.

'Amy?'

She turned and ran out of me room. Gone.

Forty-Seven

• •

We moved from Whickham. Had to.

Callum's brother put our house up for sale. Heard me mam arguing with him on the phone. But it was no use. It seems Callum never changed his will to leave anything for me mam. So much for being generous. Think his brother just wanted the money, so he could buy an even bigger place. Or maybe he just wanted revenge for what happened. Me mam had put up with all that Callum could throw at her so we could get to live in a nice house. Now it was gone.

We live across the Tyne in a council flat in Blakelaw. Think me mam had had enough of Gateshead. And, as if things couldn't get any worse, guess who was the first lad I saw in me new school? Lanky Dave. Reckoned I was in for a world of pain. But the weird thing was, Lanky Dave started chatting away like a long lost marra. I guess Amy's no longer around for us to fight over. On top of that, I think he's scared of me. If I could get me dad to kill me mam's boyfriend, he probably thought I could get someone else to kill him.

Three months later me dad got taken to the Crown Court in Newcastle. Was a day I'd been dreading. 'Specially as they wanted me to tell the court everything that had gone on. Was that nervous, I went to the toilet five times before we'd even left the house.

'Just tell them everything you told me, and the police,' said me mam.

'Aye.'

Before I went in they gave me a copy of the statement I'd made to the coppers. They let me read it. Not that I needed reminding. Everything that happened was tattooed on me brain.

I walked into the courtroom. Must be what it's like going out on to the pitch at St James' Park. All those faces looking at you. Except these faces weren't here for the excitement. They'd come to find out why Callum got killed. Everyone was there, like two sets of fans. On my side was me mam, Aunty Tina, Uncle Greg, Uncle Martin, Aunty Sheila, Gran. Also saw Megan, with a dead sad face, and a bloke I'd only seen in a photo, Uncle Connor. Then there was Callum's side, Louise, Ian, his mam, and all those whose names I still can't remember.

Went on the witness stand. Shaking like mad. They got me to read something.

'I do solemnly, sincerely and truly declare and affirm that the evidence I shall give shall be the truth, the whole truth and nothing but the truth.'

A weird-looking gadgie in a wig appeared. Think he was on the side trying to get me dad locked up. Asked me a load of questions.

Told him everything.

How mental was that? Wouldn't tell me mam one thing that was going on in me head, but here I was, in a room full of people, telling them absolutely everything.

Went right back to when Callum first turned up. Money, General, grin, grin, grin. Thought his relatives would like to hear that. Bet they wouldn't like what I was going to say next. All the stuff they didn't know, the drinking, the swearing, the battering.

Could hear some sobs. Not sure who they came from. Then I told them what I'd found out online.

Two women killed every week.

Said I didn't want me mam to be one of them. Asked the kids at school what they'd do. They all said they'd get their dad to sort it out. So that's what I did. I went to Scotland to find mine.

'How did you find your dad, Danny?'

Gulp.

Didn't want to drop anyone in it. But I knew this was the last place on earth for lies.

Hoped she'd forgive me.

Hoped me mam would forgive me.

'Me Aunty Tina told me.'

'And what happened when you got there?'

Said what a canny time I had. Apart from his fiancée running off. Told the gadgie I asked me dad to sort out Callum, and he told me he wouldn't. The end.

Questions over.

Went and sat next to me mam.

Thought she'd be mad at me. But got a surprise.

'Well done, Danny,' she whispered.

Then it was me mam's turn to get questioned.

Think it was even harder for her than me, 'cos she had to say all the things she never wanted to talk about. But I was proud of her. She told them about every single bad thing he'd ever done to her.

The prosecution gadgie said that the questions should be stopped and that Callum wasn't the one in the dock. But the judge disagreed and said that his actions were totally relevant to the case.

Exactly.

None of this would have happened if he hadn't been such a total bastard. Then me dad came out.

He had a suit on. Looked dead smart.

Sent me a little smile. Make that a wee smile.

Me dad said everything that I'd said. But in Scottish.

He pleaded 'not guilty' to the charge of murder.

Told them how he'd tracked down Callum and found out which pub he went to. Then he decided to pay him a visit.

The prosecution gadgie was a lot stricter with me dad than with me.

'Why did you travel all of the way to Gateshead?'

'To scare Mr Jeffries.'

'Did you intend to kill Mr Jeffries?'

'No, I didn't. If that had been my intention I'd have carried a weapon.'

'What we're you planning to do?'

'I was prepared to use some force to stop him hurting Danny's mam. But when I saw him staggering up the street I couldn't do it.'

'What did you do?'

'I shouted at him to leave Kim alone. I told him to get out of Gateshead.'

'And what did Mr Jeffries do?'

'He raised his fists and charged at me. So I pushed him away.'

'Did you punch him?'

'No. I gave him a push.'

Never knew that. Thought it would take a massive punch to flatten Callum.

'Mr Jeffries was a large man. Surely it would have taken some force to push him over.'

'I used the force necessary to push him away from me. If he hadn't been drinking he may not have fallen.'

'So you picked on a man who was senseless with drink.'

'He attacked me. I defended myself.'

'Then what did you do?'

'I saw that he'd hit his head. I made sure that he was still breathing. Then I ran off.'

It sounded pretty good to me. Looked at the jury to see if they thought the same. Saw twelve blank faces staring back.

Me dad was good with his answers. Like he was ready for them. A lot better than me.

The questions dried up. Neither of the gadgies in wigs could think of anything else. Then they each took their turn to speak to the jury. One gadgie said that me dad had come down to Gateshead with the intention of killing Callum. The other gadgie said he didn't.

The jury were sent out to make their minds up.

We all went out while they had a think what to do.

Outside Newcastle Crown Court, everyone stood around mumbling. Callum's lot stayed away from me and me mam. Not sure they knew what to say, giving us keep-away looks.

After what she'd heard in court me mam went straight over to Aunty Tina.

'How dare you?'

'How dare I what?' went Aunty Tina.

'Give Danny Steve's address.'

'He told me he wanted to write to him. I had no idea he'd gone to see him.'

This seemed to take the wind out of me mam's sails.

'How did you know where he lived?'

'I was best mates with her, remember?' said Aunty Tina, looking over at a lass smoking a tab.

'His sister, Rachel,' said me mam, following Aunty Tina's eyes. 'Oh, yeah, I remember her only too well. The one who brought Steve to that party.'

'I got his address from her, in case you ever needed to get in touch with him about Danny.'

The two sisters looked out across the murky Tyne.

'Why didn't you tell me, Kim?'

Me mam said nowt. Just watching the river.

'I knew something was wrong that Christmas,' said Aunty Tina, watching a bit of driftwood float past. 'You didn't return my calls. You wouldn't meet up. Why didn't you just pick up the phone and tell me?'

Me mam looked crushed. Now everyone knew that she'd taken everything Callum could throw at her – jokes, swear words, fists. And for what? A detached house with four bedrooms and a giant telly.

'You've no idea what it was like, Tina.'

Aunty Tina held me mam tight, and they both started crying.

'I didn't want to have to rely on you any more,' said me mam, through the sobs. 'I just wanted something for Danny. I thought it would all be better.'

After a long hug me mam and me aunty separated.

Me mam finally smiled.

'I'll call you.'

'That would be good,' said Aunty Tina.

She gave me mam a final kiss on the cheek and walked off.

While me mam was thinking about what her sister had said someone else came up, an older woman with scuffed shoes and a tab on the go. She stood there looking at me. Couldn't make out whether she was sad or angry or both. Thought maybe she was one of Callum's lot.

'What do you want?' said me mam, looking at her.

'Just wanted to have a good look at me grandson,' said the woman.

It was me dad's mam.

Me mam didn't know what to say next. But Stevie's mam did.

'Like father, like son,' she said.

Then she stamped her tab into the pavement. A big guy came over and put his arm around her. It was Uncle Connor.

'Come on, Sheila,' he said, in his big Scots voice.

He took her away, but not before giving me the evil eye. He'd promised me dad's mam that he'd keep Stevie out of trouble, and now I'd just landed him in more trouble than he'd ever had in his life. No wonder Uncle Connor looked like he wanted to kill me.

'What did she mean, Mam, "like father, like son"?'

Me mam watched her go. 'Nothing, son, nothing.'

We stood leaning against the railings as the brown water inched slowly towards the sea, never to see the Toon again. Wondered when me dad would next see it. Found out three and a half hours later. The jury came up with their verdict.

On the charge of murder – 'not guilty'. On the charge of manslaughter – 'guilty'.

Me dad got sentenced to four years.

Forty-Eight

• •

Me mam and me don't really talk much about what happened. We'd both said all that needed to be said. Callum's gone now, and no amount of words is going to bring him back.

She doesn't seem as mad with me as she used to. I reckon she knows that I didn't do it to hurt her. I did it to try to save her. Think she misses Callum in a weird sort of way, but she doesn't go on about him, and she's not been looking for anyone else on her computer. Think she's had it with blokes.

Didn't like being on this side of the river, away from me mates and all the places I knew. But the thing I missed most was Amy. At night I closed me eyes and looked at her face, and I thought of all the times we'd spent together, her body pressed tight close to mine, our lips locked together like soft magnets. And although I'd promised myself that I wouldn't cry no more, sometimes I couldn't stop myself, and I wet the pillow.

But a month after the court case, something happened.

'Danny, there's someone here for you.'

Me? Nobody came to see me. Not any more.

Went to the door.

Amy.

Couldn't have been more shocked if it was me dad standing there.

'Hi, Danny,' she said, smiling.

Amy didn't have any make-up on, but she still looked belter.

'You gonna invite me in?'

'Why aye.'

We went and sat in the kitchen. Me mam went somewhere else.

I wanted to grab Amy, hold her, kiss her, but I didn't. Still not sure what she'd come for.

'I went to the court.'

'You were there?' I said, flabbergasted.

'Aye, I wanted to hear what went on.'

'I never saw you.'

'I pulled me coat right up over my face. Sat way at the back.'

Probably just as well I didn't know Amy was there. Was bad enough with all those eyes on me.

'I still think you did a really stupid thing, Danny. Especially not telling me. But I know why you did it.'

Dead happy. And also dead confused.

'So why didn't you come round sooner? The court case was ages ago.'

Amy looked at the floor, like people do when they're looking for words.

'I spoke to me mam and dad about it. I said I wanted to see you again. They both said, "Over my dead body".'

'But you're here.'

'Yes, I'm here. I couldn't stop thinking about you, Danny. I really missed you.'

She stood up and we hugged like we never wanted to let go.

Amy was back. And this time I'd make sure I told her everything.

We meet up at weekends, and go as far from Gateshead as we can afford – Whitley Bay, Durham, South Shields, Tynemouth, wherever. History repeating itself. Just like me and me dad up in Edinburgh, making sure that nobody spots us.

Amy tells her mam and dad she's seeing her mates. Which isn't the biggest lie in the world. I tell me mam the truth. She's not bothered. She thinks Amy's good for me.

I sleep better now that it's all over, but sometimes I lie awake in bed at night and think about everything that happened. I think about Callum. Dead. Then I think of Megan lying in her bed in Scotland, me dad in his cell, and me mam in the room next door. Everyone on their own – because of me.

I've got me own bedroom. It's a bit rank compared to me old one, but there's a few things in it that make me happy. There's a fifteenth birthday card from Amy covered in kisses, the stone I got from the top of that stupid hill, the football from Edinburgh, the Scottish five-pound note, and last, but not least, a picture of me dad. No one seemed to have a proper one, so I got one out the paper of him outside Newcastle Crown Court. It said: *Edinburgh Man Guilty*. I tore that bit off.

But the most important thing of all is in me bottom drawer. It's something I never thought I'd get, but I did. Me mam gave it me. It's a letter from Durham Prison. She didn't want to read it, but I did.

Dear Danny,

I know I said I'd never write to you, but I guess things are different now.

I've had a long time to think about what's gone on and I wanted to tell you how I feel. It's been pretty tough for me, but I'm sure it's been pretty tough for you too. I'm not sure Megan's going to stick by me. She's visited a couple of times, but it's been hard for her. Her parents don't want her to come down. I wouldn't blame her for never wanting to see me again.

Which brings me on to you.

Part of me wants to hate you for what you did. I was just starting to get my life in some sort of order when you showed up. But I'm not going to blame you. You were just trying to help your mam, and you thought I was the only person you could turn to. I was the stupid one for doing it.

Don't beat yourself up over this, Danny. What's done is done. I should never have come down to Gateshead, but after you came to Edinburgh I couldn't stop thinking about you and what you'd said. I couldn't bear the thought of you in that house, with your mam's boyfriend doing that stuff and you lying in bed every night, scared witless. That's why I did what I did. I just wanted to frighten him away. Like most things in my life it went wrong. But I want you to know this

Danny, I didn't do it for your mam, I did it for you.

If Megan goes I'll have no one else. I doubt if anyone will bring you to see me, that's why I'd love it if you'd write, and tell me what you're up to. Are you and that girl still going steady? Are you still a world champion at crazy golf? How's your skimming arm? Been up any big hills lately? I won't be in here for ever, and when I'm out I promise to try to be a proper dad to you. I promise. And you try and be a good lad

Love you,
Stevie, your dad xx

P. S. Remember to keep your head down when taking penalties.

Even though I've read it a million times it still makes me guts go funny.

It was dead hard to track down me dad, and there are times I wish I hadn't. But when I read his letter I'm glad I did. I just wish I'd gone to see him and not asked him to sort out Callum. Should have called the police or the domestic abuse people or the council. Should have spoken to Amy. Somebody. But too late for all that. You can't turn the clocks back.

I want me mam and me to be waiting for me dad when he gets out. It's not the sort of trip I'll take Amy on. Once he walks out of the gates I'll hug him dead hard and we'll jump on a train and go to the coast. Me mam will find out that me bad dad isn't so bad any more. Then we'll find a fish shop, and eat cod and chips, talking, and laughing, and making plans. Then we'll go for a walk along the beach. I'll take me ball and we'll all have a kick about, and me mam can try running again. Then I'll find some stones and we'll have a world skimming championship. Then we'll just flop down on the sand and look out to sea, and for the first time ever it will be the way it was always meant to be.

Me mam. Me dad. Me.

● ● ●

Acknowledgements

•

A great big Geordie thank-you to me agent, Davinia Andrew-Lynch, me publisher, Fiona Kennedy, and me wife, Jann.

MALCOLM DUFFY

London, September 2017

National Domestic Abuse Helpline

If you or someone you know has been affected by
the issues raised in this story, you can contact the
Freephone 24 Hour National Domestic Violence
Helpline, run in partnership between Women's Aid
and Refuge, on

0808 2000 247

At Zephyr we are proud to publish books you can read and re-read time and time again because they tell a brilliant story and because they entertain you.

That's why we've launched the Zephyr Review Crew. We'd like to hear about the things you love in our books and what you think we could do better.

Join our review crew and be the first to read the very best new books. Members will receive exclusive author content and chances to win signed books. Just drop us a line at hello@headofzeus.com

@HoZ_Books

HeadofZeus

www.readzephyr.com

ZEPHYR